The Lord of Heartbreak

CLAUDIA STONE

DEDICATION

For Joseph, a wonderful friend and a fabulous English
teacher.

CONTENTS

ACKNOWLEDGMENTS

As ever, many thanks to my wonderful husband Conal
and our three sons for all your support.

1 CHAPTER ONE

The whole of the *ton* was in agreement that it was the love story of the season. Miss Emily Balfour had not taken two steps at her coming out ball when her eyes met with those of Julian Deveraux, Viscount Jarvis from across the crowded ballroom. Those present on the night swore blind that every guest there fell silent in that instant, as though sensing that the epic meeting of two perfect souls had just occurred.

Matchmaking Mamas watched with surprise as the previously recalcitrant Lord Jarvis danced attendance on Miss Balfour for the whole of the evening. He danced not once, not twice, but thrice with the dainty debutante, whose hair was as bright as spun gold and whose smile lit up the room. After the final strains of their last dance of the night ended, many a knowing eyebrow was raised: it appeared that Lord Jarvis, the seemingly untameable rake, had finally fallen in love.

The next day, which was a Thursday, he called on Miss Balfour at exactly eleven o'clock. He was spotted on her doorstep by a member of White's who was out taking his morning ambulations around Grosvenor Square. The pot-bellied Lord, upon sighting the Viscount, instantly forgot about his walk and instead hurried to the club to wager a bet on when Jarvis would propose to youngest Balfour girl. His entry into the famous betting book in White's initiated a flurry of similar wagers and soon the male half of the *beau monde* was watching the couple's every move with an exaggerated interest that matched their female counterparts'.

On the Friday the pair were again seen together, driving on Rotten Row in the Viscount's sleek, new Phaeton. They were accompanied by Miss Balfour's mother, who was said to have been positively preening at the attention from the crowds. On Saturday, at Lady Jersey's annual midnight ball, Miss Balfour again danced twice with the Viscount Jarvis; the quadrille and the waltz. She also stood up for two dances with a dashing young man named Captain Black, which set tongues wagging. Could it be that Emily had transferred her affections elsewhere already, people whispered with dismay. On Sunday reports circulated that several footmen bearing towering bouquets of hothouse flowers arrived at the Balfour residence after Emily had returned from Sunday Service, and at this news another flurry of betting erupted in White's. The book was closed a few minutes after Lord Payne, who was the Viscount's closest confidant, wagered one thousand pounds that Jarvis would propose the next day. There was much grumbling about one so close to the Viscount being permitted to place bets, when they were so obviously privy to insider information, though this ceased when Monday passed without news of any betrothal.

Tidings of the engagement came instead on Tuesday, in an unofficial whisper from the Viscount's butler, who shared the tidbit of gossip with the next door neighbour's footman. The footman promptly told the housekeeper, who informed the Mistress's Lady's Maid, who then took it upon herself to tell the Lady of the house. She, of course, told her husband, who promptly hurried to White's, to check the book and see who had won what was now an astronomical sum of money. And so, on Wednesday, when the official announcement was printed in the papers, there were few in London who could proclaim to be surprised by it, for even the bottom dwellers in the Seven Dials knew that the Viscount was to marry Miss Balfour. Though despite the lack of surprise everyone was still overjoyed: Who could not but be happy at the news that two beautiful, young people would be joined together in marriage?

Well, perhaps there was *one* person…

Jane Deveraux stiffened in her seat as she heard the front door of the Berkley Square townhouse slam loudly. This was then followed by her new sister in law's voice, loudly complaining to her mother about the decor of the front hall of the Jarvis's London residence.

"It's positively medieval," Emily's whining voice drifted through the door of Jane's private sitting room,as loud and clear as if there was no door between them. Jane took off her spectacles and massaged her temples at overhearing this latest complaint from her new sister. Berkley Square had been built in the mid eighteenth century and while the decor of the house might be dated, it was most definitely not *medieval.* Classical Rococo would be a more historically accurate description, but unlike Jane, the new Viscountess Jarvis had little interest in history or accuracy— or anything bar gossip and ballgowns.

"And where *is* the sister?"

Mrs Balfour did not try to keep her voice down as she spoke to her daughter, her tone laced with barely disguised animosity as she queried as to Jane's whereabouts. Jane herself stilled, her heart racing erratically; since her brother had married she had begun to feel like a criminal in her own home. Emily and Julian had returned from Cornwall to Berkley Square two weeks after their wedding, and the new Viscountess had wasted no time in letting Jane know that her presence was not wanted, and would *not* be tolerated for very long.

"Oh probably stuck with her head in a book somewhere," Jane heard Emily sniff disdainfully, "Honestly, no wonder she's a spinster— men detest women with notions of intellect."

"There's nothing less attractive than a Bluestocking," Jane heard Mrs Balfour agree with her daughter, before both women's voices receded as they ventured further down the hallway.

"Oh, goodness," Jane whispered, pushing her chair back from her writing bureau. She stood up and began to pace the small sitting room, overcome by a sense of nerves and agitation.

"Is something the matter?"

Belinda Bowstock, who was employed as Jane's companion, looked up from the stockings she was attempting to darn; the same ones she had been attacking with a needle for nearly a fortnight. Jane glanced at the young, blonde haired woman, trying to mask the fit of giggles that were threatening to erupt. Emily's first act as Viscountess had been to find Jane a paid companion, as though Jane were a woman approaching her dotage and not a lady of eight and twenty. Belinda had arrived at the house two days later; she was a dreamy girl with an artistic temperament, whose scatterbrained ways exasperated Emily as much as Jane's studious inclinations did.

"Did you not hear them?" Jane asked wondrously, for the two women had been standing just outside the door and their voices had been as clear as if they had been standing in the room.

"Hear who?" Belinda blinked in confusion, setting aside the stockings which were thick with lumpy cross-stitches and patting Henry, her King Charles Cavalier, affectionately on the head.

"Oh," Jane ran a distracted hand through her hair, marvelling at Belinda's wonderful ability to be oblivious to everything going on around her. "Never mind. I've finished the last of the corrections on my paper, shall we get ready to leave?"

The only upside of having a companion, which really *was* quite humiliating for a woman of her age, was that Jane was free to go wherever in town she pleased, without consulting her brother. Belinda happily followed Jane to circulating libraries, museums and philosophical saloons, without so much as raising an eyebrow. A different, more serious, companion might have raised an objection to attending such unladylike events, but Miss Bowstock did not seem to realise, or care, that Jane's interests fell far away from the dictated past-times that ladies were supposed to enjoy. If her miserable attempts at cross stitch was anything to go by, Jane supposed that Belinda's interests also lay elsewhere.

The two ladies quickly readied themselves and soon they were in one of the Viscount's carriages, headed in the direction of Bloomsbury. Jane held in her hands her paper on the moralities of the Romans, which she had been invited to present to a small audience at Montagu House. She nervously smoothed the sheaves of pages, reading the words aloud to herself as the carriage made its way through the busy London Traffic.

"You seem nervous," Belinda observed, tearing her gaze away from the window and glancing at Jane curiously.

"I am nervous," Jane replied, exhaling and inhaling in a manner that she hoped would steady her nerves, but instead only left her feeling dizzy and light headed. "I have never spoken in front of such a large crowd and the members of the Historical Society are *very* distinguished gentlemen."

"Well they obviously think very highly of you, if they have invited you to speak." Belinda said with a shrug, "For most men don't seem to think that women should speak at all, unless it is to offer vague comments on the weather and hair ribbons."

Jane blinked at the astuteness of Belinda's statement. Most men *didn't* think that women should talk, or hold opinions, or give presentations of historical research papers. Perhaps the young woman was right, that she did not have anything to be nervous about, for if the men of the Historical Society had not wanted her to come, they simply wouldn't have invited her.

After a half an hour's journey, the carriage drew up outside the front door of Montagu House and the footman quickly opened the door to allow the two ladies out. Montagu House was a grand affair; three stories high, seventeen bay windows wide and had a Mansard roof with a dome at the centre. Jane gulped at the grandiosity of it, though tried not to let the imposing building of the Museum intimidate her.

I have been invited, she reminded herself sternly as she swept up the front steps and into the main atrium of the Museum.

"Miss Deveraux," Sir Edward Smirke, a rotund man in his late fifties, came forth to greet Jane and Belinda as they entered the cavernous hall. "We are so pleased that you could make it. The members have been very eager to hear you present your paper. Albert Ruddhall has said that he has been corresponding with you on it for many months."

"Thank you," Jane replied with a bright smile, trying not to stammer with nerves. "And thank you for asking me to come today. It is an honour to be asked to speak with such distinguished historians."

"The honour is ours, Miss Deveraux," Smirke replied with an extravagant bow, before gesturing for the two women to follow him inside the hallowed halls of the museum. The two ladies trailed a little behind Sir Edward as they followed him to the auditorium. The hallway was one of the grandest that Jane had ever seen, with domed roofs carved with ornate Roman frescoes and heavily gilded portraits of grumpy looking gentlemen lining the walls.

"This used to be the home of the Duke of Montagu,before

the British Museum purchased it." Jane whispered to an open-mouthed Belinda, who seemed struck dumb at the grandeur. She knew very little of the girl's past, only that she had been born into a genteel family which had suffered great poverty after her father's death.

"Lud," Belinda breathed, gazing up at the dozens of chandeliers, which lead like a trail of breadcrumbs down the hallway, "Imagine how difficult it is to clean all those."

Jane blinked as a small stab of shame filled her at Belinda's words; she would never think of a thing as trivial as cleaning when she saw a chandelier, because she had never had to clean one. It was strange how two people could view the same object and be struck by totally different thought processes because of the family they had been born into.

"Here we are ladies," Sir Edward said, interrupting Jane's philosophising, a smile stretching his thick moustache. Jane wondered if it tickled, it was so big and bushy. "The members are all seated, so I will introduce you and then you will take to the podium."

"Wonderful," Jane replied, trying to quell the colony of butterflies that had erupted inside her stomach.

Sir Edward pushed open the heavy mahogany doors and led Jane and Belinda into a small, circular room, ringed by seats which were filled with most serious looking men. Sir Edward descended the steps, to the small podium at the centre and gave Jane a flattering and florid introduction that made her beam with pride. This was followed by muted, polite applause from the audience, except in one corner, where a gentleman gave a cheer more suited to a horse-race at Ascot.

Jane started and glanced to where the noise had emanated. Her face paled as she caught sight of the man who had cheered; it was her brother's closest friend: James Fairweather, Lord Payne.

What on earth?

She tried not to look at his handsome, smiling face as she took to the podium to begin her short lecture. Lord Payne was one of the *ton's* more notorious hellions. He adored women, wine and carriage races -- occasionally all at the same time if the rumours were to be believed. He had never once, in all the times that Jane had spoken with him, expressed any interest in history, or anything at all past the usual male interests of horseflesh and...flesh of another kind. She could think of no good reason for Payne to be here, unless he was up to some kind of mischief. Steadfastly she decided that the only way to deal with Lord Payne was to ignore him completely, so she turned her attention to the rest of the audience, her back to the corner where the blonde Marquess sat.

"The excavations of Herculaneum in the middle of the last century, unearthed a veritable feast of murals and frescoes which gave an extraordinary insight into the morality of the Romans," Jane began, her voice starting low and shaky before she became comfortable with speaking to the room. "From the studies of Wincklemann, who applied empirical categories upon the findings, it has become easier to analyse the behaviours of the Romans — which ranged from devoutly religious to extremely base."

"Oh-ho," Jane heard Lord Payne exclaim to the elderly gentleman beside him, "Now this sounds like my kind of history."

Jane gritted her teeth and willed herself not to glare at Payne; luckily the men seated around him, hushed him and tutted in disapproval and he was mercifully silent for the rest of her lecture. Jane focused her attention on the other members of the audience, who reassuringly were nodding and taking notes as she spoke, and who began to clap politely when she finished.

That went well, she thought with relief, before a shout of "Bravo" from Lord Payne startled both her, and every other member of the audience. Lord Payne was on his feet, his tall frame towering above the other men who had remained seated, clapping enthusiastically and seemingly oblivious to the bemusement of the other audience members.

"Well done Miss Deveraux," Sir Edward said, as she descended the podium."You've gained such fascinating insights from all your studies, it was most interesting. And some members seem to have been *overcome* with enthusiasm for your chosen subject."

Sir Edward glanced at Lord Payne, who was pushing his way through the crowd to get to where Jane stood.

"I did not know that his Lordship was such a great fan of history," Jane said with a blush, hoping that Sir Edward would not associate her with the wild, young man and think less of her because of it.

"Nor had I," Sir Edward stroked his moustache thoughtfully, glancing between Jane and the approaching figure of Payne. "His father has paid for his membership since the Marquess' first days in Oxford, but this is the first lecture that Lord Payne has deigned to attend."

There was a twinkle in Sir Edward's eye that Jane did not like, not one bit. He seemed to be insinuating that Payne was interested in more than history, which was, of course, preposterous. Lord Payne was infamous for associating with only the most beautiful of the *demimonde,* and his fiery affair with the Italian actress Marina Fusco had acted as fodder for many a gossip. He would have very little interest in a woman like Jane; from her mousy, brown colouring, to the spectacles she wore at the end of her nose, every part of Jane was the total opposite to what would attract a man like Payne.

"There you are Jane!"

Lord Payne's achingly handsome face broke into a charming, boyish grin as he finally reached his target. To Jane's dismay, Sir Edward hastily excused himself with a knowing wink, and she was left alone with the heir to the Dukedom of Hawkfield, who seemed even more buoyant than usual.

"Lord Payne," she said stiffly inclining her head. She gazed past him to the crowd, hoping to sight Belinda, who might save her from what promised to be a torturous conversation, but she was nowhere to be seen.

"She's gone into the pottery room," Payne offered helpfully, as he noted Jane scanning the room. "She seemed to be looking for somewhere to freshen up; hopefully she'll not mistake the Greek pots for chamber pots!"

Lord Payne gave a guffaw of laughter, which was quickly silenced by Jane's face, which had flamed red at his most inappropriate comment. Most men did not discuss chamber pots with ladies, even in a joking manner, though Lord Payne's grasp of etiquette had always been tenuous at best.

"I'm sure she'll realise her mistake soon," Payne offered gamely, after an awkward pause.

"Perhaps in a decade or so," Jane whispered in reply, her cheeks still red. Belinda could be gone for hours, she had very little sense of place or time and was inclined to be distracted easily. Jane wouldn't be surprised if the poor girl somehow ended up trapped in a Greek Urn. "I did not know you were a member of the Historical Society, Lord Payne."

"Nor did I," the Marquis ruffled a hand through his tawny locks, so that they fell charmingly across his forehead, as was fashionable. Jane felt a strange urge to reach out and push the lock of hair that was falling into his eyes back, though resisted, feeling slightly queer at the butterflies that once again erupted in her stomach at this most unusual thought.

"In fact I had quite forgotten it even existed until an invitation arrived for your lecture," Payne continued cheerfully, "And it was such a fortuitous coincidence that I couldn't resist attending."

"Fortuitous in what way?" Jane looked at Lord Payne

suspiciously.

"Well," the devil had the decency to blush, "I was rather wondering if you'd do me the great honour of becoming my betrothed?"

2 CHAPTER TWO

"Your what?"

James Fairweather, Marquess of Payne and heir to the Ducal seat of Hawkfield felt himself blush, as Jane Deveraux, his friend's younger sister, stared at him with incredulity. Her slightly scolding gaze reminded him of the governess he and his sister had shared as children, who had spent most of her days reprimanding the young Lord in her charge for his many misdemeanours. *I rather should have explained myself first, instead of diving straight in and proposing,* he thought wryly as he observed Jane's pale, shocked face, and silently cursed his impetuousness. Mind you, it was this same act first, think later, style of living that had gotten him into his current predicament.

"No need to look so horrified," he mumbled, his pride slightly wounded by the look of complete and utter horror on Jane's face at hearing his marriage proposal . "It would only be temporary, until I get a few things sorted out with my father."

His father, the current Duke of Hawkfield, who had been threatening to disown him for the past month.

"Please, my Lord," Jane said with a sigh, taking off her spectacles and massaging her forehead with her free hand.

"Please explain to me why you wish me to become your *temporary* fiancé?"

Jane replaced her spectacles and blinked at him quizzically. The glasses magnified her eyes, so that it felt like he was speaking with an endearing, woodland nymph, or a lost fairy, and not a lady of the *ton*. Her hand had left a small smudge of ink on one of her temples, and for an odd second James felt the urge to reach out and wipe it away with his hand. This strange impulse left him dry mouthed with shock and overcome with another queer feeling that he could not identify, so that he was unable to answer her question for almost a minute. A minute in which she stared at him as though he had three heads and not just the one.

"Well," he cleared his throat nervously, glancing around the auditorium, which mercifully was now nearly empty. "It's just I've gotten myself into rather a bind."

Well, numerous binds, if truth be told.

The disastrous Phaeton race on Rotten Row, the summer just gone, had been the start of it. He had destroyed his new vehicle in a crash that was witnessed by dozens, then read about by thousands in the papers the next day. This had been swiftly followed by more articles in the broadsheets, this time detailing the end of his affair with the famous actress Signora Fusco —which had ended even more disastrously than the Phaeton race. His lasting memories of the Italian seductress included an enormous bill for damages to the suite of rooms she occupied in Grillon's Hotel, a black eye that still pained in cold weather and a father that was infuriated by his son's ever extravagant financial affairs.

And then he had lost that damn bet at White's…

"A bind?" Jane quirked an eyebrow, and James silently cursed. He was going to have to go into details; if he knew one thing about Jane Deveraux, it was that she was a woman who loved facts and figures.

"It's actually all your brother's fault," he replied, somewhat mutinously. "For he swore blind that he would be proposing on the Monday, and then he didn't."

Jane's plump mouth twitched with a mixture of amusement and disapproval at this statement. James found himself momentarily transfixed by this involuntary action of her lips; he had not noted before just how luscious her mouth was.

"You can't blame Julian for your misfortune, my Lord," she replied, heaving a great sigh of annoyance. He was used to that sound, her exasperation, for when he had spent the summer in St. Jarvis with Julian and his sister, Jane had often seemed to find his presence a little irritating.

"Though I would not put it past my brother to have deliberately misled you for his own amusement," she continued, casting him a look that was almost piteous. Jame's heart leapt with hope—pity might make her more inclined to agree to his plan.

"Well deliberate or not, it's got me in an awful lot of bother," he replied, adopting a hang-dog expression. "I was summoned to an audience with my father, who has promised to disinherit me if I don't settle down."

"So why don't you just settled down?" Jane quipped dryly, "Why the need to pretend that you wish to marry me?"

"Because Hawkfield thinks settling down involves marriage," James replied hotly. He could feel the tips of his ears burning with annoyance as he recalled his father's dictat that unless he wed a suitable, young lady of good breeding, his allowance would be severed with immediate effect. His threats to disinherit him were easy to dismiss — for there was no other male to inherit the title but James— but cutting off his allowance was very much in his father's power. And as the man himself had pointed out, he was in excellent shape and health for a man of five and fifty and James could not hope to come into the title any time soon.

"What's so wrong with marriage?" Jane's expression was

mild, though the corners of her lips twitched and he knew that she found the whole thing rather amusing. "Your father is right, in that it's high time for you to settle down. You're thirty years of age, my Lord, are you not?"

"Yes, I am," James responded through gritted teeth; Jane was not the first person to have mentioned his age in the last few days, and it was beginning to grate on his nerves. "It's just that the *urgency* that my father has imparted upon me settling down, means that there's no time for me to look for a suitable girl, get to know her adequately enough and fall in—"

He stopped speaking abruptly, his face now burning with embarrassment.

"Enough time to fall in love?" Jane's expression as she finished his sentence was openly kind. If James had declared to any of his acquaintances in White's that he was in any way romantically inclined when it came to marriage, he would have been unmercifully mocked for the rest of his days. Luckily his slip of the tongue had happened in front of Jane, who, even though she openly found him irritating, was one of the softest souls he had ever met.

"Well, yes," he confessed, his blue eyes meeting her brown, hoping that she would see the pain that this whole situation was causing him. "I know it's not the most fashionable of ideas, but I was rather hoping that I'd find a wife that I love, and who loves me back, and that we could—"

"Live happily ever after?"

James nodded, noting the queer, misty eyed expression that Jane was regarding him with. He tried hard to resist punching the air in victory; it seemed baring his soul to Miss Deveraux might work in his favour and sadly he was not above exploiting her pity for his own gain.

"That's all very sweet and endearing, but I'm afraid I can't get involved in such an audacious lie, my Lord. It's a ridiculous plan."

"Oh."

James felt all his hopes come crashing to the ground. Jane's tone was both strict and firm, rather like a schoolmistress's'. Even the admonishing look she was giving him over her spectacles put him in mind of a governess, scolding a naughty child. He found himself bristling at her censure, as she had pointed out he was thirty years of age, which was two years older than her — *and* he was the next in line to a Ducal seat. How dare she make him feel like an unruly schoolboy, and she hadn't even let him get to the part of the plan that would be beneficial for *her*.

"I would, of course, be offering you financial renumeration for your time," he continued, in a tone that he hoped was both suave and commanding. "Your brother has informed me that he intends to sell the boarding house in St. Jarvis that you hold so dear. The Refuge for Recalcitrant Daughters, is that what it's called?"

"No." It was Jane's turn to bristle now, her cheeks pink with indignation. "As you well know, my Lord. Mrs Bakers' Boarding House is not a hideaway home for sulky teens, it is a place where young women may stay and explore their talents, academic or otherwise and not be hindered by the constraints that society so often places on them."

"Well, no one will be staying there, once the lease is up," James snorted, taking slight pleasure in the look of anger which flashed across Jane's features. "For your brother intends to sell, once June arrives and Her Grace's hold on the place expires."

The Duchess of Everleigh had purchased the lease on the famous Cornish boarding house the previous summer, after she had fled from her new husband, believing him to be a charlatan and a murderer. The Duke and Duchess were now reunited and living in almost nauseating wedded bliss on the Duke's own Cornish estate, but Olive had refused to relinquish her hold on the guest house. She had left Polly Jenkins, her friend, in charge and much to Lord Jarvis's dismay, the boarding house had remained full of eccentric, intellectual types throughout the summer.

"When did he tell you this?" Jane's brown eyes narrowed suspiciously behind her spectacles.

"Just last night, in White's," James met her gaze with a *faux* thoughtful look, as though an idea had just struck him. "I don't suppose you'd like to purchase it, and keep the late Mrs Bakers' dream of a feminine intellectual utopia alive?"

"You know very well that I wouldn't have the funds for that kind of thing, my Lord."

"But I would."

A silence fell between the two, who were faced off like a pair of boxers in a ring. Jane's pale face was flushed with anger, her eyes almost sparking with fury at his teasing tone. For his own part James tried to adopt a more neutral expression, though the memory of how she had dismissed his proposal still rankled. Which was ridiculous, as it was all a charade, but still his pride was wounded and it left him feeling defensive.

"If you agree to pretend to be my betrothed, just for the season, I can buy you the boarding house, Jane, and gift you a sum of money that would support you for many years. Think of all the young ladies you could save from the drudgery of ton life. "

James almost felt that he could see the cogs and wheels of Jane's brain whirring inside her head. He knew that since her brother had married, that Jane's position within the household had become slightly perilous. He had never been one to listen to idle gossip, but when the Viscount had announced his engagement to Emily Balfour, something his own sister had said, as a throwaway comment, had stuck in his head.

"I pity poor Jane, having to live under a mistress who is a decade her junior, it will be humiliating," Caroline had said as she read the announcement in the paper. It had caused

James to pause, and consider his friend's plight, and when his own situation became perilous he had thought of a way he could solve both their problems.

Jane had gone from being the Mistress of Jarvis House and looking after her brother's affairs, to an underling of the new Viscountess, whom James had met on several occasions and had taken an instant dislike to. He hated the thought of Jane— proud, kind, clever Jane— having to take orders from Emily, who was at best vapid and vain, at worst cruel and spiteful in the way that only very young, beautiful girls could be. Why couldn't she see that he was offering her a way out of Jarvis House?

"No one would believe it, my Lord," Jane finally replied, nibbling on her plump bottom lip nervously. "Least of all my brother, he would know straight away that it was a lie, for I'm not—I'm not—"

"Not what?"

"Not your type."

"I wasn't aware I had a type," James retorted in surprise; he adored women, all kinds of women. Tall, small, thin, curvy —he had never met a woman that he couldn't find a single attractive feature in, for the feminine form was usually beautiful no matter what way it was presented.

"You do," Jane shook her head fiercely in disagreement, as though she knew him better than he did himself. "You're always rumoured to be in the company of beautiful, scandalous, temptresses and I…I am so plain. Nobody would believe that you had fallen in love with me, my Lord."

"You're not plain, Jane," James silently cursed at his unintentional rhyme, for it sounded silly to his ears. "Whatever makes you think that? You're a smashing looking girl and clever to boot."

"There's no need to lie to try and sway me, Lord Payne," Jane sighed deeply, running a frustrated hand through her lustrous, brown locks. "Julian has told me often enough that I'm plain and that I've made it worse by reading so many books and wearing spectacles."

"Hold on, just one second," James held up a hand to silence the woman standing opposite him. "I spent much of my adolescence fantasising about women with spectacles. There's something very alluring about a woman with glasses, and there's many a young blood who uses the image of a woman like you as fodder for—as fodder for—"

James stopped speaking abruptly, his face crimson with embarrassment. Good God, had he just been about to indulge Miss Deveraux with tales of teenage boys' fantasies about their old governesses and how they acted upon them? Nobody wanted to hear that, least of all a lady of gentle breeding like Jane. Perhaps his father was right, and that he was a hopeless case?

The lady in question was gazing at him curiously, expecting him to continue with his most inappropriate line of conversation. James cleared his throat awkwardly, deciding that now was probably the best time to finish their business, before he humiliated himself any further.

"Despite what your brother has told you," he said, feeling irritated with the Viscount Jarvis for undermining Jane's confidence so, "There are many men who find women just like you incredibly attractive. On top of how pretty you are Jane, you are also clever, kind and warm hearted —and I think that most people would wonder why *you* had considered to accept the proposal of a dunderhead such as *me*. Will you consider my offer, at least a little bit?"

"I will think on it, but I make no promises." Jane relented, turning away from him at the sound of a nearby door slamming shut. Jane's companion —James wasn't certain of her name—emerged into the auditorium looking more than a little bit flustered.

"Is something the matter Belinda?" Jane called,upon seeing how scattered the young, blonde girl appeared.

"Nothing, nothing," Belinda replied absently, glancing

back at the door she had just come through, as though expecting someone to have followed her. Belinda barely glanced at James, instead focusing on Jane, her face anxious as she spoke. "Are you ready to leave?"

"I am if you are," Jane said and with a curt nod to James, whose eyes she could not quite meet, both young women fled the auditorium, leaving the Marquess standing forlornly on the same spot for a few minutes, as he pondered how on earth he was supposed to get out of his current predicament without the help of Jane Deveraux.

3 CHAPTER THREE

"Where on earth have you been all afternoon?"

Emily's voiced, laced with irritation, called out loudly as Jane and Belinda let themselves into the hallway of the imposing, three-story Berkley town house, just as the clock in the hallway was striking five.

"Jane was giving a lecture in Montagu House," Belinda responded cheerfully, oblivious to Jane's furious motions to remain silent.

"A lecture?"

Emily arched an eyebrow with such disdain as she made her way down the hallway to them, that Jane felt herself shrink under her censure. Which was ridiculous, as Jane was a decade older than the young woman before her, and not a debutant fresh out of the school room. She was allowed some leeway in her activities; after all as Emily kept pointing out, she was a veritable spinster, and spinsters never did anything scandalous.

"Yes," Jane struggled to remain composed in the face of such icy fury, "A lecture. I was invited by Sir Edward Smirke himself. It was quite the honour."

"I wonder if your brother will think it was an honour too?"

Jane who had been holding Emily's gaze defiantly, blinked at the mention of her brother. Julian would not find any pride in his sister having been asked to present an historical research paper—quite the opposite in fact. Ever since they were children he had resented how she had excelled at academics, whilst he himself had struggled. The schoolmasters that their parents had hired to tutor him in mathematics and the languages had found Jane a far more talented scholar than her brother, whose abilities were best suited to outdoor activities and sports. It was a childish thing, but Julian still resented Jane for her gifted brain, though she readily forgave him each slight and irritated sigh, for he was the only family she had left.

"Are you going to tattle on me?"

If Emily was going to behave like a child, then Jane sadly decided that she wasn't above lowering herself to the same standards.

"I'm not a tattle tale," Emily responded, with such ferocity that Jane almost laughed. Her brother's new wife was still, at heart, a child and the school-yard insult seemed to have rankled her.

"I know you're not," Jane adopted a placating tone, "Forgive me. You seemed eager to speak with me?"

"I wanted to make sure that you wear something fetching for dinner, for Mama has invited a guest. Nothing too drab, Jane dear…if you can manage that."

Emily gave a small smirk and turned on her dainty slipper, quietly sashaying back up the hallway to where ever it was she had come from. Jane felt her stomach drop; who on earth was visiting that would require her to look fetching? The slight tension she had felt since Lord Payne's unexpected proposal doubled as she wondered what her sister in law was up to now. From the smug look on Emily's face, her plan somehow involved Jane.

"Let us have a quick cup of tea to refresh ourselves, before we dress for dinner," Jane whispered to Belinda, before leading her down to her small sitting room and ringing for a maid. She threw herself into the worn, overstuffed Queen Anne chair by the fireplace and gave a moment over to reflecting on the complete absurdity of the afternoon.

Lord Payne was mad, quite simply mad, she decided as Hattie the maid, scurried into the room and placed a tray of tea and crumpets on the low table in front of her.

"I hope everything went well with your lecture, m'am," Hattie said, in her cheerful Cockney voice. Jane knew that if Emily were there, that she would scold the young woman for being overly familiar, but Jane adored all the staff who worked for her brother and couldn't bear the thought of spending her days served by nameless, voiceless servants.

"It went quite well, Hattie. Thank you for asking," Jane replied, glad to have a distraction from the gnawing worry in her stomach; what did Emily have planned? She leaned forward and poured two cups of tea, one for herself and one for Belinda, who was sitting with Henry in her lap.

"She was simply marvellous," Belinda added, with a wide smile as she stroked Henry's head. "She was so brave to stand up in front of all those serious, stuffy men —and they adored her. The Marquis of Falconbridge said that he had never heard someone speak as eloquently as Jane did."

"When did he say that?" Jane looked at her companion with surprise; she had not seen Belinda in conversation with the dashing Marquis of Falconbridge, in fact she had not noted him in the audience at all she was so distracted by James Fairweather.

"I bumped into him, in the pottery room," Belinda replied, her tone overly innocent, "While you were conversing with Lord Payne. I had not known that Lord Payne was so interested in the Romans, though perhaps he finds chariot races an inspiration for his own escapades on Phaetons?"

When she felt like it, Belinda could be very quick, Jane thought with a smile, for all talk of the Marquis of

Falconbridge was forgotten as Hattie gave a small squeal of excitement at the mention of Lord Payne.

"Oh, was Lord Payne there m'am?" Hattie asked, wide-eyed with wonder. "Is he as handsome as they say? Sarah has been filling my head with tales of him, since she returned from St. Jarvis, and the papers are always reporting on his adventures."

Jane wasn't quite of the same mind as the London news rags, who had crowned the handsome heir to the Ducal Seat of Hawkfield as the ton's most adored male. True Lord Payne was exceedingly handsome, with an athletic frame that drew the eye —but he could be ever so silly and reckless. Jane actually agreed with his father; it was high time that Lord Payne settled down and lived up to his responsibilities as a future Duke.

"He was there," Jane conceded, taking a sip of her tea to mask her frown of annoyance. "Though Belinda is right, his interest in Roman history is quite superficial."

He had only been there to try and persuade Jane to go along with his ridiculous plan, and while his offer to buy Mrs Baker's boarding house was quite tempting, Jane was too level headed to agree to play along.

"Do you think he was there just to see you then, m'am?" Hattie asked, clutching her apron with excitement. Jane frowned; good gracious, where had she got that silly, romantic notion from?

"No," she replied with a warning frown, "Goodness knows what his reasons for being there were, but I won't have you spreading idle gossip about me Hattie."

Her words were a warning but her tone was soft, nevertheless the young maid bobbed a quick curtsy and hastily withdrew from the room to inform Sarah that her mistress required a bath before dinner.

"Should I join you, do you think?"

Belinda's blue eyes glanced at Jane nervously. The young woman loathed dining with Jane's brother and his wife, almost as much as Jane did herself. The evening promised to be filled with veiled barbs directed at Jane, which her brother for the most part ignored, as he seemed to inexplicably hear a choir of angels whenever his wife spoke and not the sharp words which actually poured from her mouth.

"Perhaps you would like to take your dinner in your room, Belinda?" Jane suggested lightly, "For if Mrs Balfour is to join us with a guest, it might be awfully cramped at the table."

Which was ridiculous, as the dining table comfortably sat more than a dozen people, but Belinda had looked a little pale since they had arrived back from Montagu House.

Upstairs Jane bathed in the warm, scented bath that her Lady's Maid Sarah had prepared and allowed her cheerful servant to dress her hair in a more elaborate fashion than usual.

"Hopefully this will satisfy her Ladyship," Sarah muttered mutinously through a mouthful of hairpins as she surveyed the elegant top-knot that she had created. Lady Deveraux had made one of her first priorities as Viscountess to find Jane's Lady's Maid and give her a thorough dressing down for the way that she had presented Jane to society for the past decade. Sarah had been furious, for it was Jane herself who had little interest in her appearance, not the Lady's Maid. Jane had agreed to submit to Sarah's new-found zeal for her job, mostly because she was afraid that Emily would dismiss her from her post if she didn't.

Sarah helped her dress into a velvet gown of emerald green. It had long sleeves, as a concession to the cool early spring weather and was fitted at the bodice before it flared out into a full skirt. The shape was pleasing, flattering Jane's tall, slender figure and the dark green colour complimented her brunette tresses perfectly.

"The Viscountess wants your spectacles removed," Sarah said apologetically, reaching to take them from Jane who stopped her with her hand.

"I shall remove them before I go into the room," Jane said firmly, her sureness bolstered by Lord Payne's earlier comments. Besides, if nothing else, she needed the blooming things to make her way down the stairs or she was at risk of falling and knocking out her front teeth—and then what would the new Viscountess have to say about her appearance? Jane squared her shoulders, bracing herself against the unknown forces that would meet her at the dining table.

I'm being perfectly ridiculous, she thought with a frown, but as she pocketed her spectacles and pushed the heavy, mahogany door of the room open, she felt as though she was going into battle despite her best attempts at soothing her fears.

"There you are, Jane."

Mrs Balfour, Emily's mother, managed to make it sound as though the group seated at the table had been waiting hours for Jane's arrival, when in fact the gong for dinner had only sounded moments before.

"Yes, here I am," Jane agreed, through gritted teeth, scanning the room to see who else was present. Without her spectacles everything was a blur. She could not make out the features on anyone's faces, but she knew that the fuzzy, blonde shape near the head of the table was Emily, that her brother was seated at the top of the table and that Mrs. Balfour was seated next to her daughter. The fourth figure, who appeared to be dressed all in black, was unknown to Jane. From what she could see, which wasn't much, he was a short man, with a balding pate.

"Allow me to introduce my sister, Miss Jane Deveraux," Julian said, turning to the man beside him, who pushed back his chair to stand as Jane approached.

"Jane, this is William Sneak," Julian said carefully, "Emily's cousin."

"Enchanted Miss Deveraux," William said, reaching out a hand to take Jane's and planting a rather wet kiss on it. Jane struggled to resist visibly shuddering, for it was rather like being licked by Henry, but considerably less endearing. "A pleasure, Mr Sneak," she replied lightly, placing her slobbered on hand behind her back, so that she could discreetly wipe it on the skirt of her dress. "What brings you to town?"

Mercifully Mr Sneak pulled out a seat for Jane to sit on, for she would have struggled to do it herself, she was so short sighted without her spectacles. Rather unmercifully, however, was that the chair he pulled out was right beside his and so Jane spent the first course of dinner listening to Mr Sneak talk about himself. He seemed to think that he was a rather interesting topic of conversation, for he continued to regale Jane with tales of his life all throughout the second and third course; a stuffed pheasant and a fish *bouillabaisse* respectively. Jane learned that Mr Sneak had grown up in Yorkshire and had spent most of his youth there in the company of Mrs Balfour, his favourite cousin. He enjoyed reading, cricket and bracing walks on the moores, as well any food that didn't irritate his gout. Of late, he had taken a keen interest in the Good Book, and fortuitously his favourite cousin's new son-in-law was seeking a Vicar for the parish of St. Jarvis.

"Julian will bestow the living upon you?" Jane asked wondrously.

"Yes, Joan, your brother has kindly offered me the position as the new Vicar and everything that entails — a wonderful little parsonage on the edge of the village, and ten acres of glebe land that I can farm or let out."

"My name is Jane," Jane said, absentmindedly correcting his error. It worried her that Mr Sneak seemed more interested in the perks that the living would entail, rather than the parishioners he would be ministering to.

"Oh, yes of course. My apologies," Mr Sneak said, as he wiped his mouth with a napkin. "There's only one thing that my new life will be missing."

"And what's that?"

Jane sensed, rather than saw, that her brother, Emily and Mrs Balfour had stopped eating and were instead fixated on her conversation with Mr Sneak. The room was unusually quiet as Mr Sneak cleared his throat, as though he were going to make a grand announcement.

"What I'm missing is a wife, and I was wondering dear Joan, if you would do me the honour?"

"Jane," her head was light as she again corrected his mistake; she had not given the man leave to use her Christian name and here he was taking liberties and not even getting it right. She stayed mute as she digested his shocking proposal, allowing the silence to stretch on so long that Mr Sneak gave an impatient sigh.

"It's quite an honour, for a woman of your age to have a proposal from a man of Mr Sneak's means, if you ask me," Mrs Balfour called across to Jane, ignoring the fact that, actually, Jane had *not* asked her her opinion on the matter.

"Is that why you offered him the living?" Jane whipped her head around to look at her brother, her mind whirring with suspicion.

"It was a mere suggestion," Julian at least had the good grace to sound slightly ashamed as he addressed his sister. Jane felt her cheeks burn with humiliation at the idea that her own brother would bribe a man with the promise of an income for life on the condition that he take his spinster sister of his hands. She could just picture Emily, her beautiful face innocent, as she suggested the idea to Julian. Was she really such a burden to them?

"It's for your own good Jane," Emily spoke across her husband, her voice sugary soft and piteous. "You'll never have an offer as good as this. As Mama said, you should be honoured that a man like Mr Sneak would take you as his bride. Who else would wish to marry a woman as old as you?"

"Lord Payne does."

"The Marquess of Payne?"

"Fairweather?"

Both Julian and his wife spoke at the same time, their exclamations of surprise nearly drowning each other out as they echoed through the large dining room. Jane experienced the queer sensation of feeling as though she was not in her own body, it was almost as though she was hovering above the table, watching herself as she defiantly turned to her brother and said; "Yes. Lord Payne asked me to do him the honour of becoming his betrothed and I have accepted."

It was half true; even if it was only to be a temporary arrangement, she was truthful in saying that he had asked her to become his betrothed. Jane's head was light and fuzzy and she could hear her heartbeat pounding in her ears as her brother regarded her silently. This was most unlike her —acting without thinking. Usually she considered every action she took carefully before carrying it out, but this surprise announcement had fallen from her lips without her brain even registering what she was saying. True, it had been spurred by a desire to not have to marry Mr Sneak, but also something else— a desire to prove Emily and her mother wrong: someone did want to marry her.

"Has he lost a bet?" Julian had found his voice at last.

"No," Jane retorted, ears red with indignation. "He has not lost a wager. Honestly Julian, how can you ask such a thing?"

"Because I know James," her brother replied with a snort, "And of all the ladies of the ton that he could have proposed to, you would have been at the bottom of a very long list."

Emily gave a sugary giggle at this statement and even Mrs Balfour joined in with a strained laugh of her own.

"It's just so unbelievable," the young Viscountess agreed, placing a hand on her husband's arm, "that a Marquess would want to marry you."

"Yes, I suppose, if *you* could only nab a lowly Viscount,

then it's thoroughly unbelievable that a Marquess would wish a spinster like me to be his bride," Jane snapped back, "However, James only holds the courtesy title of Marquess until he inherits, so I suppose you'll have to grapple with the astonishing fact that a man who will be a Duke wants to marry me. But don't worry sister dear, I'll only have you address me as Your Grace when we are in public."

Jane threw her napkin down on the table and pushed her chair back. She knew that she was being petty and had fallen far below her usual standards of behaviour, but she was furious. And as she stumbled her way out of the room she was overcome by the wish to be wearing her spectacles, if only so she could see the look on Emily's face. As she grappled with the door handle she heard Mr Sneak give a worried whisper; "Does this mean that Lord Jarvis won't be offering me the living?"

Jane slammed the door behind her and fled up the hallway, only pausing when she reached the stairs. *What have I done?* The enormity of the fact that she had just announced her engagement to a man she could barely tolerate was beginning to dawn on her, as well as the worrying realisation that Lord Payne had no idea that he was, in fact, now her fiance.

"Oh dear," Jane whispered as she gathered her skirts and hurried up the stairway to her room, "I shall have to find a way to let him know."

4 CHAPTER FOUR

"Did you bribe the poor girl?"

August Fairweather, Fifth Duke of Hawkfield placed his morning paper on the table with a flourish as his son entered the room.

"Bribe what poor girl?" James replied, taking a seat just to the right of his father and smiling gratefully at the discreet footman who immediately placed a cup of hot, steaming coffee before him.

"Miss Deveraux, that's who." the Duke pointed at the paper he had folded, his thick grey eyebrows arched in annoyance, "It worries me that you have so many candidates you might be bribing that you can't think of whom it is I'm speaking."

James took a sip of his coffee, before he responded, grimacing at the bitter taste of it.

"The papers were quick off the mark," was what he finally settled upon as a response. Gingerly he lifted the offending news rag from under his father's elbow and began to flick through the pages to find out what had actually been reported. He found the piece on his engagement in the society pages, a whole column dedicated to what had transpired in White's the evening before.

He had been seated at the famous bow window, staring morosely out into the rainy street below, when one of the club's footmen had informed him that there was an urgent message for him. James had taken the envelope, upon which his name was written in unfamiliar handwriting, and opened it nervously. His father had been so vehement in his criticism of him of late, that he was almost afraid the letter would be some kind of missive from King's Inns, stipulating that the Duke was to legally disinherit him. Instead, his eyes wide, he had read a simple, curt few lines from Jane, accepting his proposal.

My Lord,

I have decided to accept your proposal, please be warned that my brother is now aware of this fact. I hope you will call on me tomorrow so that we can corroborate the story of our false courtship lest anyone question it.

Yours,

Jane

"She said yes," James turned to the footman who had remained standing impassively beside him, lest he was needed, his eyes wide with shock from what he had read. "She's agreed to the betrothal."
"My congratulations, my Lord."
The footman's face had remained as expressionless as ever, for White's hired only the best, but another person had overheard James's exclamation, Theodore Blowbury, who immediately summoned for a decanter of brandy to celebrate. Once that was finished he called for another, as the night was young. Then another, and another, and James wasn't too sure, but from the pounding of his head he was almost certain that they had called for a fifth decanter to celebrate his engagement, which by that stage

the whole club was aware of. Then, he had stumbled back to his Father's London residence in St. James' Square, rather than his own bachelor abode in Mayfair, thinking to tell his parents about his impending nuptials before anyone else did.

Except his plan had gone rather awry, due to the fact that someone had obviously alerted the papers to the news and that he had not been able to drag himself out of bed before noon to get to his father before he had read the aforementioned papers.

"When did they start calling you the Lord of Heartbreak?" his father asked with a derisive snort as James finished reading the column and pushed the paper away from him.

"After the Italian broke all the mirrors in the suite Grillon's," he offered, picking up the toast that had been placed before him and liberally applying it with butter and jam. James had learned never to refer to Marina by name in his father's presence, as he was still smarting from the astronomical bill that the famous hotel had sent to repair the mirrors in the suite that had once housed Louis XVIII. And for the repair of the windows, and — actually— any piece of glassware that the fiery Miss Fusco had been able to get her hands on that fateful night.

"I broke her heart, so she broke everything else was what they said at the time. Rather witty, don't you think?" James asked through a mouthful of toast, though judging by his father's frown, he didn't find the moniker quite as amusing as his son did.

"Let us not talk of the actress," the Duke said, picking up his tea and sipping it thoughtfully, "I wish to discuss Miss Deveraux, and how it is that an irresponsible, young buck like you could persuade such an intelligent creature to marry you."

"It was just as you suggested, father, bribery," James quipped, quickly adopting a look of contrition as his father's eyebrows narrowed into a dangerous frown. "I jest, I jest. I think I simply wore down any reservations that Miss Deveraux might have had by being persistent. We spent a considerable amount of time together last summer in St Jarvis, and I think that in the separation that followed she realised that I had grown on her."

"Like a fungus," his father chuckled, pleased with his insult.

"Not like a fungus," James protested, wondering how best to phrase it, "More like a unwanted puppy that was foisted upon her, that she eventually became fond of despite herself."

It was a rather good analogy and it seemed to placate his father, who harrumphed in a way that was neither satisfied nor dissatisfied. James suppressed a groan of irritation at his father's behaviour and wondered if he too would become a grumpy, old codger when he inherited the title.

"And you?" his father glanced at him with penetrating blue eyes that were a mirror image of James's own. "What prompted you to propose? I've never known you to bother doing anything which wasn't completely self serving. Did you decide to exploit her feelings for you so that I wouldn't cut off your allowance?"

"No," James responded, with more indignation than a man lying through his teeth truly deserved to feel. "I simply realised how precarious her situation has become, now that her brother has wed and she is no longer mistress of her own house. I hated the thought of her being unhappy so I decided—"

"To rescue her?"

James had never seen his father look so startled and he had also never seen the Duke look at him with that strange expression on his face. If he hadn't known the man for thirty years, he'd almost call it pride that filled his father's eyes, but surely not; the man could barely stand to be in the same room as him and had never been proud of anything James had done.

"Well this is a turn up for the books," the Duke finally

said, pushing back his chair to stand up. He was built like his son, with broad shoulders and an athletic frame; and while, unlike his son, the Duke's middle had given over to a slight paunch in recent years, he was still in possession of a figure that most men his age could only dream of. "I didn't think it was possible, but it seems you've found something that you care for more than drinking and gambling my money away. Cherish her, son. I'll visit the Archbishop and see about having the banns read."

"The banns?" James croaked to him as he walked away, hoping that his face wasn't displaying the shock that he felt. "Already?"

His father paused at the door and turned to look at him curiously; "Well they have to be read out for three Sundays before you can marry. I rather thought you'd be in a hurry to get it over and done with."

"I am," James blustered, knowing that the tips of his ears were bright red, as they always were when he lied, "But I must speak with Jane and find out what she wants…and I have not yet spoken with her brother."

"Why does that not surprise me?" the Duke rolled his eyes in annoyance, an act that James almost found comforting it was so familiar. "And I suppose you'd best tell your mother, heaven knows she'll want in on the organising of the event."

Ah, his mother, Georgianna, Duchess of Hawkfield; she was the reigning queen of the ton and would rather make Jane a widow before she had a chance to get down the aisle, if her son did not allow her to orchestrate the most extravagant wedding imaginable. It would be loud, it would be brash, it would be the event of the season and, James realised with a jolt, it would be extremely tricky for either he or Jane to extricate themselves from their engagement once his mother got started. She was quite capable of frog-marching both parties to the altar at gunpoint in order to get her way.

"Do I have to tell her?" his voice was almost pleading; he really hadn't thought this plan through.

"Aye, you do," his father sighed, "And I shall have to write a letter to my accountant informing him of my imminent bankruptcy at her hands."

With a resigned laugh his father left the room, leaving a queasy James staring after him. When he had made his plan he had thought that nothing could go wrong with it, but now he was beginning to realise that there was one rather large problem: his parents might not allow him to break the engagement and he might just end up wed to Jane Deveraux after all.

It was well past two in the afternoon by the time that James arrived at the Deveraux's Berkely Square home. The houses on the square were all three stories, with white stone facades, each facing out onto the large gardens at the centre. James stood at the top of the steps which led to the front door, as he waited for someone to answer his knock.

"Lord Payne," a most discreet, black clad butler eventually opened the door and ushered him inside. "I apologise for keeping you waiting, there has been a rather unexpected amount of callers this afternoon."

"Really?" James raised an eyebrow at the butler's slightly flustered appearance; he supposed that the poor man had not had to deal with a plethora of visitors when it was just Jane who lived there. The new Viscountess probably had the house full of giggling, giddy debutants, for the poor man appeared exhausted.

"I have never seen so much lace, in all my days." the butler confided in a whisper as he led James to the door of the drawing room. As he pushed the door open James peered into the room with trepidation, which was justified as he took in the sheer numbers of women who thronged the large, airy room. There was at least two dozen, he surmised, perched elegantly on chaise lounges and sofas, or hovering at the periphary, all with their eyes turned toward Jane, who looked most uncomfortable at the attention directed her way.

"It's him!"

A high pitched whisper caused each perfectly coiffed head to turn in his direction and James had the startling experience of learning what an actor must feel like on stage. Forty-eight, wide eyes were staring at him, twenty four rosebud mouths opened into O's of excitement.

"Ladies," he gave a short bow and turned to Jane, "Miss Deveraux."

"Oooh," collectively every young lady present sighed as James addressed his intended; he was almost certain that the curtains had swayed from the breeze they had created with their exclamations.

"Lord Payne," Jane stood, a look of abject relief on her face. "How good of you to call. My brother wishes to speak with us in private—perhaps later, when…" She trailed off and cast a despairing glance around the room at the young ladies who were all listening to her, "Perhaps when all my guests have left."

James bit back a laugh at her obvious discomfort at having so many callers; he supposed that Jane had never been embroiled in any scandal or gossip before, and had not experienced what it was like to have to whole ton descend *en masse* seeking to be entertained.

"It's quite alright Jane," Lady Jarvis, who James had not noticed until she spoke, said in a waspish tone. "The ladies are here to see me as well as you, it's perfectly fine for you to leave."

From the Viscountess's peeved tone, it was easy to deduce that she was more than a little bit put out by Jane's new found popularity, and from the looks of irritation that James witnessed on the visiting ladies' faces it was easy to see that Emily was wrong. Everyone was there to see Jane and not the Viscountess.

"He's in his library," Jane whispered as she gestured for him to follow her to the door. James passed through the throng of ladies, whose eyes all followed his progress across the oriental style rug and followed Jane out of the room.

"Lud." Once the door was shut behind them and they were both alone in the hallway Jane visibly relaxed —he could actually see the tension leave her shoulders, which had been hunched and defensive.

"How did the papers find out so soon?" she asked in a whisper, as she led him down a small corridor, presumably toward Julian's library. "I swear, the second the clock struck noon they all descended at the same time. I have never had so many ladies call upon me —actually, I have never had *any* lady pay a call on me."

There was no hint of self pity in the last statement, only wry amusement and James felt a jolt of something wrack his body as Jane threw him a conspiratorial glace from beneath her spectacles. Her brown eyes seemed to visibly sparkle with gold when she was amused by something, it was most disconcerting.

"I suppose there are some ladies who find the prospect of marrying a Duke very glamorous," he replied stupidly for his brain had turned to mush, only wondering after he had spoken if he had sounded rather pompous.

Jane snorted at this statement and he realised that yes, he had.

"They are to be pitied then," she whispered, pausing outside a closed door. "For in the ten hours or so that we have been engaged, I have found little glamour, my Lord. Only stress and vexation."

"Have you been stressed?" A feeling almost like remorse filled him and he reached out a hand to take hers. His fingers brushed the lace trim of the cuff at her wrist, causing Jane to jump and look down at his hand in confusion.

"Only a little," she glanced up at him, nervously chewing

on her plump bottom-lip. "I said it mostly to jest, my Lord."

"You can call me by my given name, now that we are betrothed," he said in response to the weak smile she offered him.

"We're not really betrothed, though are we?" she replied in a low whisper, casting a nervous glance at the closed door. James was struck by a strange stab of something, that if he thought on it he would have realised was masculine pride, but he had never been one to think too deeply, and before he knew it he had responded.

"You are my betrothed," his voice was lower than usual, almost a growl, "And as such I reserve the right to all the entitlements that come with that. Including hearing you call me by my name."

"It's a faux betrothal," Jane whispered back, her cheeks flushed with annoyance, "We're not actually going to get married. We just need to do the bare minimum to convince everyone that it's genuine, until enough time has passed that your father is convinced you have changed your ways and one of us can cry off at the last minute."

"Oh-ho," James cried, ignoring the flapping of Jane's hands that was intended to silence him. "If you're going to keep up your end of the bargain it will require more than doing the bare minimum. You will attend every ball I attend, you will dance every dance I ask of you and you will bloody well act like you're enjoying it."

His breath was ragged as he finished speaking and judging by the alarmed look on Jane's face he must have been visibly bristling with the annoyance he felt. Which wasn't annoyance per se, more wounded pride that Miss Jane Deveraux was blatantly not enchanted with the idea of spending time with him. Which was ridiculous, for that was the very reason he had chosen her: he had wanted a fiance who would cry off at the last minute and not try to exploit their bargain for her own gain. Jane opened her mouth, with what would have proven to have been an equally angry retort, had the door for the library not opened and silenced her.

"I thought I heard voices," Lord Jarvis said, peering between James and his sister with an expression of annoyance.

"We were just about to knock, Julian," Jane replied, smoothing down the front of her dress with agitated hands. "I informed Lord Payne that you wished to speak with the both of us."

"Yes, I do."

James had never seen Julian look so churlish and he felt slightly nervous as his friend gestured for the two of them to enter his study.It was a large room, lined on three sides with mahogany bookshelves, which were packed to bursting with leather bound volumes. James wondered if his friend had actually read any of the books on the shelf, for they looked pristine, whilst his desk, where several decanters of various alcohols sat, looked much more used.

"Take a seat," Lord Jarvis said, his dark eyes narrowed as he gestured to the two sofas which sat facing each other in front of the fireplace. James waited for Jane to sit, before perching beside her; close enough so that he could feel her body trembling slightly. He felt wretched as he watched her from the corner of his eye; she was wracked with nerves and it was all his fault.

"I suppose I should have asked you first, Jarvis," James said as Julian sat down opposite them, his face a picture of brotherly disapproval. "But as Jane has passed her majority, she didn't need your blessing—though I hope you will give it?"

"I would, if I was certain that this weren't some sort of joke."

"A joke?" James glanced at his fiance in confusion; why would her brother think their engagement was a jest?

"Yes," Julian's face was red with anger, his handsome features made less so by the scowl he wore. "If this is some kind of trick you're playing Payne, intending to humiliate me in some way, then know now that I won't stand for it."

"How would my marrying your sister humiliate you?" James was flabbergasted by the accusation. He glanced at Jane for some sort of explanation, but her face was pale, her mouth a thin line of worry. "Oh," Julian growled, "I know that this is some sort of trick you're playing. Some sort of bet with all of those fools in White's. Find an ageing spinster and pretend that you're in love with her, or some such nonsense. I won't stand for it Payne, I won't let you humiliate me like this."

"I rather think the only person who's humiliating you, is you yourself, Jarvis." A dark cloud of red had descended on James's brain; he was so livid with anger at the way that Jarvis had spoken of his sister that he was fit to slam his fist into his friend's smug face. "How dare you speak of Jane like that in front of me. I won't stand for it —and if I hear any word of you belittling her or ridiculing her again, then mark my words, I will call you out."

James stood, his tall frame towering above the Viscount, who was watching him, his mouth open with astonishment. "I will have my man of business send forward the marriage contract —if you fail to understand any of the longer words in it, then I'm sure your sister will be able to explain them to you. Jane," he took a breath, to try to quell the anger that was coursing through his veins. "As ever, it has been a pleasure. My mother will be in touch about a small dinner to celebrate our betrothal."

He turned on the heel of his Hessians and stormed out of the room; past the startled butler and two ladies who were departing to their carriages, who watched him with wide eyes as he stalked out into Berkley Square. It was only when the chill, Spring air hit him that he realised the enormity of the mess he had entangled himself in. He had threatened his closest friend with a duel for the sake of a woman's honour—a thing he had never imagined himself doing. It was an act that one would associate with a man in love, which James most certainly wasn't; though he was a much better actor than he had previously given himself credit for, for if he had witnessed himself in Jarvis's library, he would have called himself a lovestruck fool.

5 CHAPTER FIVE

"Oh, dear."

Jane surveyed the cavernous dining room of Hawkfield Hall, which was thronged with people. There must have been at least two-dozen of society's most impressive people present, glittering under the light of the chandeliers. When the Duchess had sent the invitation she had included a small, handwritten note assuring Jane that the dinner would be a tiny, intimate affair where both women could get to know each other. Jane glanced nervously at the crowds of people and deduced that the Duchess's idea of intimate and her own differed vastly. She did not recognise any familiar faces among the crowd, bar Lord Payne, who was deep in conversation by the fireplace with a young, handsome man, and did not appear to have noticed her entrance. Her brother and Emily, both still thoroughly annoyed with her, had abandoned her the moment they had entered the room, leaving Jane standing in the doorway feeling rather out of place.

"You must be Jane."

A small, bird-like woman of about five and thirty stood before Jane, her dark eyes dancing with mischief.

"I am," Jane gave the woman, who looked vaguely familiar

to her, a weak smile.

"I am Caroline," the woman responded, tucking her arm through Jane's and leading her further into the room, "I'd like to say that I've heard all about you, but James has rather sprung this upon us all. I'd also like to say I'm surprised by his behaviour, but I've known James his whole life and there's very little my brother can do now to shock me—except…"

The woman, who Jane guessed was James' sister Lady Caroline, looked at Jane curiously, her head tilted to one side, like a curious bird.

"Except, I really wasn't expecting him to announce his betrothal to someone like you," she said, her brow furrowed as she surveyed Jane.

"How do you mean?" Jane asked, wondering if she should have taken Emily's advice and left her spectacles at home. It appeared that even James' own sister thought her too dowdy for her handsome, younger brother.

"Well," Lady Caroline looked a little embarrassed, her pale cheeks turning pink. "I wasn't ever expecting James to marry a woman that I would like. Oh, he's been so fond of empty headed, flibbertigibbets for years and when I heard he was engaged I was certain he would have picked a most unsuitable, green girl, fresh from the schoolroom. Then my father told me that it was you James was intending to marry and I was over the moon to hear it. Oh, I think we'll be fast friends Jane and I've always longed to have a sister. My husband Giles is involved with the Royal Historical Society and he's simply dying to make your acquaintance. Come, I'll introduce you both."

Jane found herself being led to a corner of the room where Giles Bastion, Caroline's husband stood, deep in conversation with the handsome man that Jane had seen James speaking with moments before. The introductions were made and soon Jane found herself engaged in an enjoyable conversation with Giles and Harry Dalton, who it transpired had just returned from an exploration of the

South Americas. The gong was sounded for dinner and much to Jane's relief, Caroline insisted on moving her from her original placing beside Emily, to the seat beside Harry.

"You both seem to be getting along so well," Caroline said loudly, "It would be a shame to separate you."

This statement was accompanied by a mischievous wink from Caroline, who wrinkled her nose in Emily's direction. Jane stifled a giggle; it seemed her sister in law to be was as fond of the Viscountess Jarvis as she was. *Except she's not to be my sister in law,* Jane reminded herself sternly, ignoring the guilt which accompanied this thought. She had not expected to find herself having to spend any time with James' family, when he had first proposed the idea of a fake engagement, and now that she had met Caroline, she regretted that the friendship which they would surely have formed would never come to be.

Jane smiled gratefully at Mr Falton as he chivalrously pulled out her chair for her to sit on.

"Thank you," she said with a wide smile, as the explorer took his place beside her at the table. "You really must tell me more of the South Americas. I have never known anyone who has visited, excepting an old friend, Mr Jackson —though he has not yet returned, I think."

"Are you by any chance speaking of Alastair Jackson?" Dalton asked, setting down his glass of wine and glancing at Jane curiously. Jane could have sworn that her heart stopped beating as the explorer mentioned the name of the man who had once been the love of her life.

"I am," she offered, hastily taking a large sip of her own wine to mask the sudden nervousness which was skittering through her veins, "Are you acquainted?"

"Oh more than acquainted," Dalton gave a rueful chuckle, "We're practically an old married couple after sharing a cabin on the crossing back to Bristol."

"Alastair is back in England?" Jane was so surprised by

this news that she knocked her glass of wine over, the red liquid quickly spreading and staining the pristine, white table cloth. From the corner of her eye she could see Julian glaring at her from his place near the head of the table, but she ignored him. The news that the man she had loved, or at least thought she had loved, for nearly a decade had returned to English soil was so all encompassing that she did not care for her brother's censure, nor that she may have made a rather *large faux* pas in front of the Duke and Duchess.

"Why did he return?" she asked hurriedly, absently blotting at the wine stain with a napkin. "He told me that he would be gone for five years at the least."

Alastair was an ornithologist and had left England the previous summer on an expedition to study the native insects of South America. He had also left Jane completely heartbroken at having been abandoned in favour of centipedes and larvae, after ten years of waiting for him to propose.

"He was bitten by a nasty spider of some sort,' Dalton grimaced, "He nearly died. Had to have two toes amputated and the cost of the treatment ate through his funds for the rest of the trip. He was quite ill for a lot of the journey, though he picked up as we neared home — said he was looking forward to meeting up with a lass he had left behind."

Jane, who had just lifted her soup spoon to sample the white soup which had been place before her, dropped the piece of cutlery on the floor with a loud clatter as she heard this rather startling piece of information.

"Oh, I am sorry," she whispered, her face red as she accepted a new spoon from a footman who had leapt into action at the commotion she had caused. She could feel several pairs of eyes, her brother's the most annoyed, watching her, but she chose to ignore them and refocused her attention on Bastion, who was tucking into the heavy, creamed soup with gusto.

"Did he mention which lass this might be?" she asked; her voice, which she had tried to keep light and casual, came out as a strangled whisper.

"A girl in Cornwall, I think," Dalton replied, looking at her curiously, "Do you know her?"

Jane mutely shook her head and turned her focus to the bowl of soup before her. Her mind was reeling from this second revelation: Alastair was still interested in her. She wondered if he had gone straight to Cornwall, where her family's estate lay in the quiet enclave of St Jarvis, or if he would come straight to town? Perhaps he would call on her this week, she thought excitedly. As her bowl of soup was removed and replaced with a platter of red-meats dressed with herbs, Jane glanced up and caught sight of James, who was seated on the opposite side of the cavernous dining table, a few seats to her left. His face wore a frown of concern as he watched her, his blue eyes tender and kind.

He probably thinks that I am dropping spoons and spilling drinks because I am nervous, Jane thought, with an ache. How could she tell Lord Payne that it was the news of the return of the man she had once dreamed of marrying, that had made her so clumsy?

Somehow Jane made it through the next seven courses without any more outward mistakes, helped by the fact that she diverted all conversation with Harry Dalton away from the topic of Alastair Jackson. She encouraged him to tell her tales of the jungles, rivers and tropics that he had explored and he was such a charming, interesting story-teller that she was shocked when dinner ended and the Duke announced that the menfolk would be retiring to his library for a spot of port.

"It was so wonderful to speak with you, Miss Deveraux," Bastion said with a smooth bow before he departed. Jane smiled warmly and stood for a moment as she watched him follow the trail of men who were hastily departing the dining room.

"You and Dalton seem to have hit it off."

"Oh," Jane turned at the sound of James' voice and gave him a slightly shocked smile; she hadn't realised he was still there. "He's a very interesting man, your sister insisted we sit together."

"I'm sure she did." Lord Payne scowled across the room at his sister, who simply gave him a lazy wave, "She's always been good at making trouble."

Lord Payne's face wore a dark scowl which contrasted with his light colouring and was so opposite to the cheerful demeanour that he usually wore.

"I don't understand how seating me beside Mr Dalton would cause any trouble?" Jane responded, feeling more than a little perplexed by the statement; did James somehow know his connection to Alastair?

"Well, you were talking to him; for the whole evening I watched you talk to no one but him," James huffed, frowning down at her.

"Of course I talked to him," Jane almost laughed at his ridiculous statement, "It would have been far worse if I had sat beside the man and ignored him completely."

"That's not the point," James argued, ignoring her perfectly rational response, "My sister sat you beside him to try to invoke feelings of jealousy in me at watching my intended swooning over another man, all night long."

"I was not swooning over Mr Dalton," Jane responded, issuing James with a glare of her own. "How dare you accuse me of such base behaviour. And there is no need to feel jealous of Mr Dalton. We are not actually engaged, if you remember, and he and I were simply having an interesting conversation—he's an interesting man."

"And I'm not?" James asked, his voice low with annoyance.

"Usually you are, my Lord," Jane replied, exasperation finally taking hold, "But tonight you are acting like a mad-man and you will excuse me, I have to join your mother and the other guests in the drawing room for tea."

Jane pushed past her betrothed, anger simmering in the pit of her stomach. Caroline stood waiting for her in the doorway, her eyes alight with amusement.

"Was that a lover's quarrel I witnessed?" she asked, glancing pointedly at her brother who was still standing in the spot where Jane had left him, anger radiating from his very being.

"No," Jane sighed, feeling worn from James' ridiculous attack, "You simply witnessed the beginning of your brother's descent into madness. Can you believe he accused me of swooning over Mr Dalton? I have never swooned in my life."

"Did he?" Caroline's dark eyebrows shot up in wonder, "I have never known James to feel jealousy toward any man. My, my —he must be thoroughly smitten with you."

"He's not—" Jane stopped herself before the dry, sarcastic comment that Lord Payne was not smitten by her, in any way, rolled off her tongue. They were supposed to be head-over-heels in love; she had nearly forgotten that they were engaged in a charade and that she had a part to play.

"Oh, don't be so modest," Caroline linked her arm through Jane's and led her into the drawing room, where Georgianna, Duchess of Hawkfield was waiting impatiently for them, "I've never seen a man fidget like that through so many courses. Honestly at one stage I thought he was going to launch himself at Dalton and throttle him with the trout."

Jane lamely joined in with Caroline's giggles, her mind reeling with confusion. Lord Payne was not in love with her, he was simply playing a part, like she was. The news of Alastair's return had her wondering, however, if she might be giving up her acting career before it had truly begun.

6 CHAPTER SIX

The next day, just after noon, James found himself once again standing on the doorstep of Jane's Berkely Square residence, this time with a bouquet of hot-house flowers in hand. He waited impatiently in the chill Spring air for someone to open the door. He had been wracked with guilt all night for his ridiculous behaviour with Jane after dinner and wanted to apologise. Preferably sooner rather than later, for he was anxious to explain to Jane that his annoyance wasn't flamed by jealousy, rather by his sibling's mischief making. He had known Caroline his whole life and she had always relished in goading and provoking him, as only an elder sister could. Not for the first time in his life James wished that Caroline had been born a boy, or at the very least born younger than him. She had always seemed one step ahead of him, seeming to know how he would react to something before he even did.

"Lord Payne," the butler opened the door, peering around the huge bunch of roses which was obscuring his view to offer James a smile of welcome.

"I have come to call on Miss Deveraux," James said, inhaling a sprig of gypsophelia as he spoke, which left him coughing and spluttering in a most undignified manner.

"I'm afraid Miss Deveraux is not at home," the butler replied benignly once James' coughing fit had ended.

"Not at home?" James paled; goodness was Jane giving him the cut absolute for his boorish behaviour last night? He gave the butler a curious look, wondering how informative the man would be. "Do you mean she's not at home because she has left the premises, or that she's not at home because it is I who is calling on her?"

To James' surprise the butler gave a peal of laughter, his previous impassive expression exchanged for one of wonder.

"I beg your pardon, my Lord," the butler hastily apologised, once more donning a staid face, "But that is the second time today that I have been asked that question, I have never in all my years working for Miss Deveraux experienced as many callers as I have these past few days. Miss Deveraux is not at home because she has gone to call on your mother with Lady Jarvis. Would you like me to take the bouquet and put it in water?"

"Yes, please," James replied absently, passing the monstrous bunch of flowers to the man and following him inside the door. His mind was mulling over what the servant had said about him being the second person to ask the same question—who else was there that thought Jane was avoiding them?

"I'll just leave my card," he said casually, striding over to the half-moon table, which stood under an ornate, gilt mirror. Upon this table was a very showy calling card box, with an engraved ivory lid. James extracted his own card from its case in his breast pocket, before lifting the lid to place it inside; before he did however, he stole a glance at the card which lay on the top of the pile. Instead of reading Harry Dalton, as the raging, jealous beast in his chest had suspected, it read: Mr Alastair Jackson, Ornithologist. The card gave an address in Bloomsbury, which James duly noted, in case he needed to call on whoever this chap was at a later date. He had no idea who this Jackson fellow was, or what an ornithologist was for that matter, but Jane had some explaining to do.

"There you are darling, what a surprise to see you up and about so early." Georgianna, Duchess of Hawkfield's voice positively boomed across the vast drawing room to her son as he entered. James resisted rolling his eyes at his mother's theatrics; she was not a woman who did anything quietly. Indeed, even her dress was loud. Today she wore a large turban of turquoise, topped with an ostrich feather which bobbed as she turned her head. Her dress matched the colour of her turban and an opulent necklace of sapphires glistened at her neck. She looked much younger than her fifty years, though next to Jane, dressed in a simple, dove grey dress, she looked rather flamboyant for so early in the day.

"I was just asking dear Miss Deveraux to regale us all with the tale of how you both fell in love," his mother continued, waving a hand to encompass Lady Jarvis and his sister Caroline into her plans. Lady Jarvis wore a sour look on her face that made James think that being regaled with their supposed love story was the last thing she wished to experience.

"I'm finding the time line of your courtship rather difficult to understand," his mother continued blandly, gesturing for James to sit on an empty chair beside Jane. "It seems you have known each other for months, though there is no urgency on Miss Deveraux's part to march you down the aisle. Can you try to persuade the girl that no one wants to wait until December for a Christmas wedding? I'm barely able to wait until the Bishop finishes reading the banns!"

Jane cast a despairing look at James, her eyes pleading with him to stop his mother before she sent for a Vicar to perform the nuptials there and then. The Duchess was a formidable woman at the best of times, but when she had her heart set on something she was as dangerous and calculating as the Duke of Wellington himself.

"Now, Mother," he said carefully, knowing that he needed to word his response carefully. "I shall not have you overriding Jane's wishes, whatever she wants she may have."

"Well," Georgianna huffed, "I'll just have to convince Jane that what she wants is actually what I want. Won't I Jane, dear?"

Caroline, who was seated beside the Duchess, looked visibly alarmed at her mother's steely tone. Jane seemed to shrink into the overstuffed chair she was seated in and merely offered the Duchess a faint "Ah" as a response, apparently to afraid to actually form a word.

"How we came to fall in love," James blurted loudly, in a desperate attempt to end the moment, "Was really quite simple, wasn't it Jane?"

Jane nodded mutely and blinked at him from behind her spectacles. Her deep brown eyes were full of worry and grey shadows ringed them. James felt a stab of guilt as he saw how upset she was; it was all his fault. Accusing her of trying to charm Bastion and then leaving her alone to do battle with his mother.

"We spent rather a lot of time together, when I went to stay in St Jarvis," he continued, ignoring the fact that he had actually been in Cornwall to hide from his father's ire after he had been publicly disgraced again. "We took walks along the cliffs, sat reading together in the library, Jane even got me to attend a lecture on the history of women's literature."

Caroline raised an impressed eyebrow to the last statement, which like the two previous was only a slight variation of the truth. The only walk that James and Jane had taken along the cliffs near St Jarvis had occurred because he had accidentally knocked her best bonnet off whilst play acting on the way home from Sunday Service, and they had both been forced to chase it before it landed in the sea. Reading in the library, for James at least, had involved the racing pages of the newspapers and much muttering about bad bets, whilst Jane absently chastised him for gambling in the first place, without looking up from the pages of whatever book it was she was devouring. He had only attended the lecture on the history of women in literature as his visit to Cornwall was coming to an end and he had wanted to see inside the boarding house that Julian was forever disparaging. Jane had been more than a little reluctant to bring him, though he had behaved himself, quite taken aback by the way the quiet, mousy woman he had lived with for months had transformed into a passionate, persuasive speaker as she delivered her portion of the night.

"We became quite accustomed to each other's company," James continued, "And when I returned to town I could not understand what was wrong with me, why I felt so out of sorts."

"You missed Jane," Caroline offered, not bothering to conceal her look of glee.

"Yes, I rather think I did," James offered his fiancé a wide smile, "And then when the invitation to attend Jane's lecture on, on—"

"The moralities of the Romans," Jane helpfully supplied, discreetly rolling her eyes at his lack of attention to detail.

"Yes that," James beamed, "My heart nearly exploded and I knew that it was because it had recognised what I had been missing all that time."

"Jane," Caroline sighed, casting a dreamy glance at Miss Deveraux who had turned a charming shade of pink at the attention. Blushing seemed to accentuate the alabaster paleness of her skin and the warmth of her chestnut brown locks. Goodness, how did I ever think she was mousy? James thought with surprise. Jane was radiant, her beauty soft and understated, the type of beauty that could go unnoticed by men who were only attracted to a loud, brash type of prettiness. Men like James.

"Well that settles it." James started as his mother clapped her hands together loudly, her voice voice firm. "It's clear, Jane, that my son is completely besotted by you and I won't have you leave him waiting a moment longer. The wedding will take place the Monday after the last banns have been read, and I won't hear any argument against it."

James stole a glance at Jane, who had paled at his mother's words. She wore the look of a woman who had been sentenced to the gallows and for some reason he felt like he had been kicked in the stomach at her reaction. You're not actually getting married, he reminded himself sternly, you have more important things to worry about, like halting this blasted wedding that you didn't want in the first place.

Everything he had planned had gone horribly, terribly wrong and he was beginning to think that what he thought he had wanted at the start of this charade was exactly the opposite of what he wanted now.

.

7 CHAPTER SEVEN

"We shall have to begin preparing your trousseau," Emily said, the moment that the two women arrived back at their Berkely Square home. "Then I shall have to make an appointment for you with Madam Le Chat, she's the only *modiste* I will allow you to attend. She can work miracles; even with you."

Jane ignored Emily's underhand barb and simply took off her pelisse and handed it to Austin the butler who was waiting patiently on the two ladies.

"Miss Deveraux you had two male callers when you were out," he said kindly as he took the light garment from her, "Both were most eager to let you know they had called. They left their cards, shall I fetch them for you?"

"Thank you Austin," Jane said with a smile, "But I am perfectly capable of walking the three steps to fetch them myself. You would have me a lazy sloth if you had your way."

"Oh, indeed, I hate to see you over extend yourself."

Jane suppressed an irritated sigh at this comment; Austin was a dear but he could be rather overbearing at times. She lifted the lid of the silver card holder and picked out the top two cards from the pile. The first was Lord Payne's, which she was expecting for he had told her that he had called whilst she was out. The name on the second card caused her to emit a gasp of shock, which had Emily watching her with narrowed, suspicious eyes.

"Who called?" her sister in law asked casually, removing her own shawl and shoving it at Austin without even glancing at him.

"Oh, just a most esteemed member of the Historical Society," Jane lied, knowing that it would halt Emily's interest.

"Oh, how dull," Emily replied, her eyes near glazed over with boredom. "I will take a small rest Jane, then we can spend the evening preparing and making plans. You will need a dozen new dresses for the season, for you cannot be seen in Lord Payne's company looking as dowdy as you do now."

With a swish of her skirts the young Viscountess made her way toward the staircase, calling for her lady's maid as she went. Jane watched her, until she was certain that she was gone, then glanced at the card again.

Alastair had called.

A tidal wave of emotions swept over her, excitement, happiness…anger. For she and Alastair had exchanged harsh words the last time that they had spoken and he had broken her heart; the heart that had beat for him for almost a decade.

"Could you please have one of the maids send some tea to my parlour?" Jane asked Austin absently. She made her way down the corridor which led toward the kitchens, where the small corner of the house that she could truly call her own was situated. Belinda was seated by the fireplace, with Henry warming her feet, a book in hand.

"You're back," she said sweetly, though her face fell when she caught sight of Jane's harried expression.

"Oh, dear," Belinda rose to her feet, dislodging Henry who gave a sigh of protest, and gestured for Jane to sit down.

"Whatever is the matter? Are you upset because of the man who sent the flowers?"

"What flowers?" Jane asked quizzically.

"Those ones," Belinda waved her arm toward the window, which was nearly obscured by the huge bouquet of red-roses and gypsophelia. It was the most spectacular bunch of flowers that Jane had ever received—actually it was the only bunch of flowers that Jane had received in her eight and twenty years.

"Do you know who sent them?" Jane asked, moving toward the window so that she could truly appreciate their splendour. The gypsophelia puffed around the roses like little clouds of baby's breath and when Jane reached out a hand to stroke one of the rose petals, she noticed a card nestled within.

"There's a card," she whispered to Belinda, who gave her an encouraging smile. With shaking hands Jane opened the envelope and gave a sigh when she read the short missive. It simply said: Forgive me Jane, I have been a fool.

"What does it say?" Belinda asked, "Does it say who sent them?"

"No," Jane read the words again, "Though I know who they are from."

Alastair: he had come back into her life and was begging for forgiveness.

"Lord Payne?" Belinda asked, her eyes alight with softness at the romance of it all. Jane felt her stomach drop at the mention of his name. How could she explain to Lord Payne that the true love of her life had returned and that she could no longer carry on with this charade of an engagement? How would she explain it to his mother, for that matter? The Duchess had been like an army general, summoning the cook to prepare menus for the wedding breakfast, the housekeeper to ensure that the ballroom would be adequate for the number of people she wished to invite and finally ordering James to visit his barrister so the marriage contract could be drawn up and signed by the day's end.

"They're not from Lord Payne, Belinda," Jane said slowly, tucking the card into the pocket of her skirts.

"Do you have another paramour?" Belinda asked, her voice breathless with excitement. To Jane's surprise she gave a twirl, before exclaiming, "Oh, this is so exciting! Perhaps Lord Payne will challenge him to a duel at dawn for your heart?"

Goodness; Jane made a mental note to check the titles of the books that Belinda was forever reading. It appeared that sugary-sweet romances had rotted the poor girl's brain.

"No one will be duelling over me," Jane assured the girl, breaking off as Hattie bustled into the room with a tray of tea and sweetmeats.

"Beautiful flowers," she commented in her cockney accent as she set the tray on the low table before the fire, "I heard you've two men chasing after you now Miss. Isn't that a fine thing. I always say men are like Hackney carriages, you can wait forever for one and then two come along all at once."

To Jane's surprise the maid gave her a rather saucy wink, before bustling back out the door, humming a cheerful tune. Good gracious, had every member of the household become afflicted with some sort of infectious disease that had stripped them of their sense of reason? What woman would want two men duelling over her? It sounded like a most exhausting predicament to be in.

Once the door was closed behind the maid, Belinda turned and looked at her curiously.

"Who is the man who sent them, Jane?" she asked quietly, "For it seems to have upset you a great deal."

For a girl who spent most of her days with her head in the clouds, young Miss Bowstock could sometimes be incredibly astute at reading people.

"He was a man I loved for years," Jane sighed, walking to

the table and pouring them both a strong cup of tea. She added a lump of sugar to her own cup for good measure; strong, sweet tea was what one needed for shock, or so Hattie always said. "He is a very intelligent man, heavily involved in the world of academics. We corresponded on various ideas for years and our friendship was the highlight of my rather dreary life until last summer..."

"Until?" Belinda prompted, for Jane had trailed off and was staring morosely at the flowers.

"Until last summer he declared that he would be leaving on an expedition for the South Americas which would take five years," Jane volunteered, "He asked me to wait for him, but I refused as I knew that to promise myself to him meant that any chance I would ever have to have children, or a family of my own would vanish."

"Quite a sensible choice," Belinda, who had possibly never made a sensible choice in her life, nodded wisely.

"Oh it was more pride on my part," Jane shrugged, giving her companion a wan smile. "I was hurt that he would favour exotic insects over me; I should have realised that a man of his passions would never be satisfied until he knew everything there was to know about his field of study."

"Which is insects?" Belinda wrinkled her nose and fed the biscuit that she had been about to eat to Henry instead. "I have never heard the words passion and insects used in the same sentence...but what do I know?"

"Alastair is an ornithologist," Jane replied defensively, slightly hurt on Alastair's behalf that his chosen profession was being mocked. "He is meticulous in his study and documentation of all classes of the insect kingdom. Why he has devised his own method of classification that has been adopted by all members of the Ornithological Society of Great Britain."

Jane paused to allow Belinda to absorb this monumental achievement, though, after a moment of bewildered silence on her companion's part, Jane had to assume that nomenclature was not a feat that impressed Miss

Bowstock.

"He sounds like a most admirable man," Belinda offered dubiously, her pretty face wearing an expression which belied her words. Jane stifled a sigh; she knew that compared to Lord Payne Alastair sounded like a dull, stick in the mud. Unlike Lord Payne however, Alastair had once felt actual feelings for her. It was hard to defend him to Belinda when doing so would reveal that her engagement to the future Duke of Hawkfield was all a charade and that Payne probably felt more affectionately toward his horse than he did to Jane. She glanced at Belinda, whose face was troubled as she pondered the predicament that Jane was in.

"I know you might think me flippant, for wanting to throw Lord Payne over in favour of Alastair," she whispered.

"I don't," Belinda protested, "It's just not like you to be so inconsiderate of someone's feelings."

Ah, so that was the crux of Belinda's issue.

"It's *not* like me," Jane agreed, and, deciding that she could take her companion in her confidence, she leaned forward and whispered; "It's just that Lord Payne and I are not *actually* engaged, you see. He asked me to pretend to be his betrothed so that his father would not disinherit him."

"Never," Belinda's eyes lit up at the scandal of it all, "Why that's quite clever."

"It was, until Alastair resurfaced and complicated it all."

Jane heaved a deep sigh at the predicament that she now found herself in; really she had lived a very simple life before James Fairweather upended it all with his silly plans.

"It doesn't have to make it complicated," Belinda suggested, thoughtfully scratching Henry's ears and feeding him another biscuit. "Presumably your plan with Lord Payne would have culminated with one of you calling the whole thing off?"

"Yes," Jane agreed, "Though we hadn't quite decided who. I think it would have been more believable for him to have caught a case of cold-feet, than I, for he is such a catch and no one would think that I would be fool enough to let such a man go. Though he was insistent that honour would not allow him to break the engagement and that I was to do the deed."

"So it is you who will break the engagement?"

"Yes, and I worry that it will cause a lot of upset to James' family, who are really quite lovely. I wouldn't want his sister to think that I am a cold-hearted witch."

"Well then," Belinda shrugged, "You have the perfect excuse - your childhood sweetheart has returned and is whisking you away to get married. It's rather romantic, she couldn't hold it against you." The blonde girl beamed at Jane who struggled to form a smile of her own to return; in ten years Alastair had never once proposed marriage, and she needed him to do it within the next three weeks for that plan to work.

"Are you over the moon that he has returned?" Belinda asked dreamily; seemingly happy to hop from one Romantic hero to another, now that it wasn't at the expense of Lord Payne's feelings. Jane thought for a moment, before nodding as a reply. She was happy that Alastair had returned, that he had apologised and that he wished to reenter her life, but she wanted the feeling that was gnawing at her stomach to disappear. The feeling of guilt— that she knew would only go once she shared her news with Lord Payne.

.

8 CHAPTER EIGHT

Normally James thoroughly enjoyed every ball he attended, for what was there not to like at a ball? The food, the music, the dancing; everything was designed for pleasure. Not to mention the chance to flirt with the fresh debutantes or, even better, any dashing widows who had always appealed to him more than the green girls who collapsed into floods of giggles at the mere sight of him.

Tonight, however, he was filled with a restless impatience as he prowled the periphery of the dance floor of Lord and Lady Thackeray's opulent ballroom. The place was thronged with guests, it was setting up to be a crush, yet despite all the people there, there was one person who was conspicuous in her absence.

Jane Deveraux.

James scanned the couples on the floor, who were engaged in a boisterous quadrille, but she was not there. He heaved a sigh, thinking to fetch himself a glass of ratafia, or something stronger if it could be found, when a familiar figure caught his eye.

"Lord Payne," the new Lady Jarvis gave a wide, cat like smile as she spotted him. She was resplendent in an off the shoulder gown of pale rose, which complimented her blonde curls and exquisite figure perfectly. She was flanked on either side by two young ladies that James did not recognise; both were extremely beautiful, in that fragile, doll-like way that had become so popular of late. They glanced at him from under long lashes, with eyes that were alarmingly calculating for such young ladies.

"Allow me to introduce Misses Gemma and Audrey Blaise," Lady Jarvis said with a smile that showed her pearly white teeth. "We were actually just discussing your forthcoming nuptials, my Lord."

"You and every other person here," James gave a modest smile. He had spent the whole of the night thus far batting off enquiries as to the big day—mostly from members of White's, who he was sure had opened a betting book—and from Society Mamas who seemed most cross with him for having taken himself out of the marriage market.

"Such an unusual pair you make," Gemma Blaise said slyly, with half-feigned innocence that was intended to let Payne know that her comment was meant as a barb.

"In what way?" James felt himself bristle with annoyance, for the impertinent young madam wasn't the first person to say that to him this evening. Honestly, for a society that was obsessed with manners and etiquette, people could be incredibly rude about women who wore spectacles.

"It's just that you and Miss Deveraux are such opposites," Audrey interjected, earning a nod of agreement from the Viscountess. "You are so outgoing and charming, whilst Miss Deveraux is so…studious."

Never had the word studious been inflicted with such negative connotations, James thought with chagrin. Lady Jarvis then spoke, before he had a chance to respond.

"Indeed," she simpered, smiling up at him, a smile that did not reach her eyes. "Even Julian has commented on what odd a match it is. He always thought that you would choose a bride who was more sociable. The Misses Blaise are quite accomplished at dancing, singing and all the more feminine arts. Julian says that if he hadn't chosen me he would have fallen in love with one of them."

Julian stared at Lady Jarvis in dumbfounded shock; had she honestly just suggested that her two friends were a more suitable match than her sister in law?

"Frankly, I've never been attracted to the same type of women as Julian," he responded in as casual a tone as he could muster. "It's a matter of taste. Excuse me ladies."

With an extravagant bow he left the trio of ladies and went in search of the ratafia that he had been looking for before he was so rudely accosted. He hoped that someone had thought to add something stronger to it by the time he got a glass. The ball was in full swing as he pushed his way through the glittering, glamorous crowds. The Thackeray's were the beating heart at the centre of the ton and every guest present was either well titled, well connected or both. In the room adjoining the ballroom, where a small finger buffet had been set out, James spotted Ruan Ashford, Duke of Everleigh skulking in the shadows sipping on a tumbler of what looked like brandy.

"I'd give my left eye to know where you got that," James grumbled, to which Everleigh gave a wry smile.

"No need to go to such great lengths, Payne," Everleigh said, giving an almost imperceptible nod to a foot man, who returned seconds later with a fresh glass for His Grace and another for James.

"How do you do it?" James asked, slightly awestruck.

"It just happens, once you assume the title," Everleigh said with a shrug, "You'll find out once you're Hawkfield, servants will be watching your every twitch to see if they're needed."

"Sounds delightful," James snorted, "What happens when you sneeze?"

"The whole of London town stops to offer me a handkerchief," Everleigh replied, "Well not really, but sometimes it feels like it. Sometimes holding a Ducal seat feels like being an exhibit at the Pantheon Bazaar, you'll learn that hiding in the shadows is sometimes more preferable when you inherit."

James took a swig of brandy, savouring the way it warmed his throat, and contemplated this advice. He already felt like the world watched his every move as the heir to Hawkfield. He couldn't possibly imagine the interest and curiosity getting any worse.

"You made a sound choice, in Miss Deveraux," Everleigh continued, his eyes on the guests in the room beyond. "You couldn't find a better woman to help you cope with the endless duties that accompany the title."

James followed the Duke's gaze to where Jane stood beside Olive, Duchess of Everleigh, deep in conversation and oblivious to the guests who were milling around them, trying to bask in the pair's reflected glory. His heart gave a strange leap at the sight of her; she was dressed differently tonight. Her hair was piled atop her head in a charming disarray of curls and her dress, while not as ostentatious as the other ladies present, clung to her curves in an understated way that left him rather dry-mouthed. Since when had Jane Deveraux possessed an hour glass figure that would make a tavern wench envious? James watched as his betrothed threw her head back in laughter at something the Duchess had said and he felt a stab of envy toward Olive; he wanted to be the one to make Jane laugh like that. The thought hit him like a runaway carriage— was it possible that he was interested in Jane romantically? It would make sense; the jealousy he had felt at seeing her with Dalton, the address of that Jackson chap that was seared into his brain, the protective way he felt toward her. He had said to his father that he had wanted to take Jane away from her miserable life with her brother, and he realised that it was true. He wanted Jane Deveraux as his wife, not his fake fiance.

"Thirsty?" Everleigh asked with an arched eyebrow, as James threw back the rest of his tumbler of brandy.

"I have things to do," he replied mysteriously, departing

with a curt nod and heading in Jane's direction.

"Oh, there you are." Jane blinked at James in shock as he elbowed his way through the crowds to her side.

"Jane," he took her hand and bestowed a kiss on it, before turning to the Duchess to acknowledge her, "Your Grace, how nice to see you in town."

"I wish you could say that it's nice to see my husband too, but I seem to have lost him to a decanter of brandy," Olive replied with a grimace, she turned to Jane and wagged her finger, "I know that everyone will tell you there's no man better to marry than a Duke, but appreciate the time you have with Lord Payne before he inherits and turns into an irritable old crank. It seems that to hold a Ducal seat one must hold the ability to be both obstinate and ornery all at the same time."

Although her words were irritated there was affection in them and the Duchess soon departed in search of her husband, though not after promising Jane that she would call on her the next day.

"It seems I will be making a lucky escape, my Lord," Jane offered with a smile, "For Dukes sound like a rather obstreperous breed of men."

"Oh, I don't know," James shrugged, feeling a little befuddled to find himself alone with Jane now that he knew himself to be in love with her. "My mother seems to manage my father alright."

"I think the Napoleonic wars would have ended in a week if your mother had been in charge," Jane retorted lightly, with a smile that rendered James dumbstruck with desire. How had he not noticed before the way that her eyes twiinkled so charmingly when she bestowed a smile upon him?

"A dance," he stuttered after an awkward pause in which Jane gaze distractedly over his shoulder, "You have promised me as many dances as my heart desires."

"I did not, my Lord," Jane grinned modestly, a note of humour in her voice. "I promised you as many dances as was necessary to uphold my end of the bargain."

"And you haven't even given me one," James mockingly chided, holding his hand against his chest as though his heart was broken. "A man of lesser confidence might think that you were avoiding it altogether."

"Luckily you're a man whose confidence could only be described as overflowing," she retorted quickly, her words softened by her gentle smile. James felt his chest swell slightly; it was nice to think that he was giving the impression of being confident and assured, when in actual fact he now felt like a stuttering schoolboy in her presence. The small orchestra in the far corner of the room had finished the final strains of a boisterous country-set and were now preparing to begin to play a waltz. Lord Payne instinctively held out his hand and was rewarded when Jane held out her own, interlinked her fingers with his and allowed him to lead her out onto the dance floor. The room hushed slightly at the sight of them together, for this was their first public appearance since the news of their engagement had been reported. James felt the inquisitive eyes of the ton watching them carefully, but he did not care, for he had eyes only for Jane. As the first strains of the music started, he placed a hand on her waist and pulled her toward him; a small bit closer than propriety allowed, but it was worth it for the heady rush of desire that almost left him dizzy.

"I must confess, my Lord," Jane whispered nervously, glancing at him, then over her shoulder at the people watching them, "That I have never danced the waltz in public."

"Really?" he asked in surprise; he had danced dozens, if not hundreds, over his lifetime.

"Well it is a rather romantic dance," Jane reasoned, nervously following his steps, "And I have never really been anyone's romantic interest at a ball."

"Well, tonight you are mine," James replied in a croaky whisper, pulling her closer again.

"Yes, well, if only for show," Jane smiled up at him. Before he had a chance to reply she spoke again, her cheeks flushed with pleasure. "I know that we have not properly discussed the way that we shall end our engagement, but I think I have a plan that even your mother could not thwart…"

As they continued dancing Jane explained in a whisper about the return of her former paramour Alastair Jackson. James listened with a sinking heart as she described their decades old friendship, which was strengthened by their shared love of the academics and now Jackson's return from the South Americas.

"Don't you see?" Jane asked, her eyes dancing with a happiness that sent spears of jealousy through James. "I can cry off at the appropriate moment without anyone suspecting that it was all just a charade. It would have looked odd — and your father would have been suspicious— if Alastair had not returned and given us the greatest excuse. It's wonderful!"

"Yes, marvellous," James replied gruffly, feeling as though fate were playing some sort of hideous trick on him. Perhaps it was retribution for all his past misdeeds and rakish behaviour, that he finally thought himself in love, only to find that the woman who had stolen his heart had already given hers to another. The dance ended and one by one the couples began to drift off the floor. James stayed for a moment, with his hand still resting lightly on Jane's waist.

"The dance has ended, my Lord," she said with a bemused smile.

"It has," he agreed, giving himself a mental shake to wake him from the fog of confusion that had clouded his mind, "But it was only the first Jane, there will be more."

Hundreds more, he vowed silently, for he would not allow this Alastair Jackson steal Jane away from him.

9 CHAPTER NINE

"Oh, Jane, this is just the type of room I always picture you in when I think of you!" Olive, Duchess of Everleigh said as she followed Jane into her private parlour the next day. The Duchess prowled the room, curiously trailing a finger over the spines of the books which were crammed to bursting on the shelves which lined three of the room's walls. She gave a happy sigh as she took in the vast collection of leather bound volumes, and the odd ornaments and curiosities that Jane had collected over her lifetime.

"It's warmer here, than in the drawing room," Jane said as Hattie came bustling in with a tray of tea and a plate full of buns. "Though I know I should probably be hosting a Duchess in the grandest room of the house no matter how chilly it is."

"Oh, hush," Olive rolled her green eyes in annoyance, "Honestly, I'm still the same person I was before I married Ruan. I'm still the woman who served you tea and bread I'd baked myself last summer."

Hattie gave a subtle nod of approval as she heard this, causing Jane to smile. Olive was one of the most easily likable people she knew. The Duchess was practical and hardworking, having grown up with a father who often lost the family's fortune gambling. Airs and graces were not something that Olive would ever affect, even though her title gave her leave to do so.

"Belinda," Jane spoke to her companion who had been standing awkwardly since Olive's arrival, wearing a look of terror on her face. "Allow me to introduce the Duchess of Everleigh. Olive this is Belinda Bowstock, my companion."

"Your Grace," Belinda was so startled at actually having to speak to the Duchess, that she dropped Henry, who she had been holding in her arms, and gave Olive a sweeping curtsy more suited to an audience with the King.

"I beg you," Olive reached down to pick up Henry, who looked rather disgruntled at his unexpected tumble to the floor, "Call me Olive. I did not know that you had hired a companion Jane?"

This last statement was delivered with a note of confusion, which caused Jane to sigh.

"I did not," she said huffily, as she poured tea into three china cups. "Emily insisted that a lady of my advanced years would need company and so she hired Belinda. And it's not that I am not glad of your company Belinda," she added, so as not to offend the girl. "It was just quite insulting that my new sister thought me old enough to require you."

"The new Viscountess sounds most charming," Olive said, with a hoot of laughter, accepting the cup of tea that Jane proffered with both hands. "She is quite young though, is she not? I recall thinking that women of my age were positively at death's door when I was eighteen. Though now I'm nearly thirty I think I was a little hasty in my assumptions."

"She is but eighteen," Jane agreed, thinking that Olive was right and that she should allow Emily some concessions for her age. "And I almost feel pity for her, for she seems in such a rush to assume the airs of an older woman. She has not had a chance to appreciate her youth —she didn't even have a full season before she married."

"Unlike some of us," Olive said with a wink to Jane, "Who took a bit longer to find a man who met our expectations. Now, enough about Emily —I want to hear all about your Lord Payne. Do you know, when I first heard I thought it wouldn't work as he is much too silly for you. Though, after seeing you together last night and the way that he looks at you so adoringly, I'm happy to say that I was completely and utterly wrong. He's smitten by you."

"Is he?" Jane asked, shocked by Olive's statement. She had not realised that she and Lord Payne were such convincing actors, though she rather thought that Olive was simply imagining things, carried away by the false love story they had peddled society. There was no way that James Fairweather, he of beautiful widows and seductive actresses, was looking at Jane with anything other than barely disguised boredom.

"Oh, yes," Olive nodded, scratching Henry's ears. The King Charles gave a growl of pleasure, perfectly pleased with being pampered by a Duchess. "Why, even Ruan commented on how Payne could not take his eyes off you —and for Ruan to comment on anything that isn't a horse or a ship is rather something."

Colour crept over Jane's cheeks as she heard this and a feeling of pleasure began to grow inside her like a tiny shoot warmed by the sun. Quickly she squashed it, for it would do no good to start thinking that Lord Payne was interested in her; he wasn't called the Lord of Heartbreak for nothing. And besides, she told herself sternly, Lord Payne was not the type of man she was attracted to. He was too charming, too handsome, too much of a rake, for her tastes. True, he was kind, exceptionally kind, but far too boisterous for a woman like her.

"I think that you and Everleigh have been reading too many Gothic Romance novels, Olive," Jane replied modestly, "For Lord Payne's decision to wed is rooted in practicality. His father had threatened to cut off his allowance if he did not change his ways —and what better way to prove he was reformed than to align himself with a sensible woman like me."

"What do you mean?" Olive's eyes narrowed dangerously. "Is he using you in some way Jane? I don't know why you'd agree to marry him if it's just so he can hold on to his allowance and continue to drink and gamble his way across town once you are wed.'

"No, no," Jane protested crossly, "It's not like that at all - we have no intention of actually getting married, the whole thing is just a ruse to buy Lord Payne some time."

"A false engagement?" To Olive's credit she did not look like she disapproved, instead her face wore a thoughtful look. "I don't quite understand what you gain from the arrangement Jane?"

"The boarding house in St Jarvis," Jane supplied reluctantly.

"Of course," Olive laughed, "I should have known that nothing except that ruddy house would tempt you to act so rashly."

"It wasn't just the house," Jane protested, feeling a little annoyed at Olive for not understanding the multiple layers which had compelled her into agreeing to Lord Payne's scheme. "When he first told me about his plan I told him that he was mad —which is still my personal opinion on the whole charade. However, Emily and Julian decided at the same time as Payne made his proposal that I would wed her horrid cousin and live my days out in St Jarvis as a Vicar's wife."

"Oh, dear," Olive sighed, "I had not realised. You should have known that you could have come to me and Everleigh —you are always welcome in our home Jane."

"I know, and I thank you Olive, but I am nearly nine and twenty and I don't wish to be beholden to anyone for my living —I want a home of my own."

A silence filled the room as Olive digested these words; Jane knew that out of anyone the Duchess could empathise with her need for independence. Olive had initially fled her marriage to the Duke, thinking him a murderer, to set up a home in St Jarvis. True, they had been reunited and had fallen madly in love with each other, but the gleam in Olive's eyes let Jane know that she understood what it felt like to feel utterly helpless and alone in life.

"Well," Olive clapped her hands brusquely, "I can't blame you for wanting your own independence and at least Lord Payne isn't the actual cad that the papers portray him to be. The only thing I'm concerned about is his mother."

"You and me both," Jane said, taking off her spectacles and massaging her temples to soothe the headache that was threatening. "She has already begun planning the ceremony, the wedding breakfast, my dress…"

"It will be hard to extricate yourself from all that," Olive advised sagely.

"Yes, but, and this is the most exciting part," Jane perked up, realising that she had not yet told Olive the good news. "Mr Jackson has returned from his expedition to South America and is very eager to take back up our acquaintance."

The silence which followed was deafening. Olive's mouth was tight with disapproval and she seemed to actually be biting her tongue —an act that Jane had always thought was just a figure of speech. She saw a flash of curiosity cross Belinda's face and the young woman glanced subtly between Jane and the Duchess, trying to assess what had caused so much tension.

"So, like the insects he has spent so long studying, your Mr Jackson has crawled out from under a rock and is trying to worm his way back into your affections?"

Jane was rather taken aback by the ice in Olive's voice. She placed her glasses back on and blinked curiously over at her friend, who was tapping her foot impatiently on the floor.

"Whatever do you mean?" Jane asked with confusion.

"What I mean," Olive replied, "Is that I overheard your last conversation with the cretinous Mr Jackson and if you had any ounce of pride you would tell that stuffed-shirt, pompous prig to get straight back on the next boat to South America and leave you alone."

Jane flushed, with both annoyance and humiliation; the last time that she and Alastair had spoken cruel words had been exchanged by both parties. For Olive to judge him on one, short conversation—that she had been eavesdropping on—was absurd.

"I think you're taking a rather harsh view of Alastair," Jane said defensively, ignoring Belinda who was now outright ogling the exchange with wide eyes. "He has apologised. Just look at the beautiful bouquet that he sent."

She gestured to the window where the bouquet still stood, the flowers as fresh as the day that they had been delivered. Jane knew very little about flowers, having received just that one bunch, but she was sure that Alastair must have spent a fortune on them —and he was not a wealthy man.

"He would have to plant you a rose garden bigger than Hyde Park before I'd consider forgiving him," Olive snapped, her face falling as she realised how harsh her tone had sounded. "Oh, Jane, I'm sorry. I'm just so annoyed with him —you're far too good for a man like Alastair Jackson."

Jane remained silent, though she was slightly mollified by Olive's apology. It was all well and good for a woman like Olive to have such pride, she thought glumly. Olive was beautiful and vivacious, with auburn hair that quite literally turned heads when she walked into a room. While, as Julian so often said, the phrase plain Jane seemed to have been invented just for her. Alastair had been the first man to see past her dowdy appearance and fully appreciate her for her mind.

"Let us not argue," Jane finally said, reaching out for the pot to pour another cup of tea, "I want to hear all about everything that has happened in Cornwall since I left and how Polly is getting on at the boarding house."

The rest of the morning was then spent discussing local gossip and Polly Jenkins, Olive's friend who now ran the boarding house in St Jarvis. They talked for nearly an hour, until the Duchess finally declared that she must take her leave.

"Please promise me, Jane," Olive said as Jane walked her to the door, "That you won't act in haste and will think hard before you decide to meet with Mr Jackson."

"I will, I promise," Jane lied, stepping heavily on Belinda's toe before she gave the game away. For that afternoon they were set for a lecture on lesser known larvae in Bloomsbury, and Jane was fit to burst with the excitement of it all.

10 CHAPTER TEN

There was nothing better for clearing the head than a hard ride on a chilly morning, James thought as he leaned low against his stallion's neck. Hyde Park was near empty at this time of the day, the deserted fields partially obscured by a light fog. James urged his horse into one last spurt, relishing the way his muscles ached from the exertion as well as the thrill of the speed. He slowed down to a gentle canter as they neared the proper riding paths, to allow Inglot to cool down, for both horse and rider were covered in a sheen of sweat from the vigorous exercise. James held the reins loosely in his hands, his mind elsewhere as he made his way along the quiet bridle path. His mind was so far away, in fact, that he did not notice the rider approaching him until he called out a greeting.

"Good morning, my Lord. You're up early."

It was Harry Dalton, the explorer. His handsome face wore a friendly smile that James could not help but return. Now that he knew that there was no romantic connection between Dalton and Jane, he was more inclined to be friendly to the fellow.

"I like to get a good ride in before the crowds start to gather," James explained, drawing Inglot to a halt, so that he could speak more with Dalton.

"Yes, nothing ruins a good gallop like some ninny deciding to dash across your path," Dalton agreed with a good natured smile. "I must say, I enjoyed myself immensely at your engagement dinner. Your father was so kind to invite me, after his generous sponsorship of my last exploration. I must congratulate you on your choice of bride also, my Lord. Miss Deveraux is quite something —so well read and intelligent."

James felt a stab of pride at this comment, which was faintly ridiculous as Jane wasn't actually intending to wed herself to him, so he could not really take any pride in her having chosen him.

"And what a coincidence that she knew Alastair," Dalton continued blithely, unaware of the interest that James had in that particular name.

"Alastair Jackson, the ornithologist?" James tried to keep his voice casual, when really he wanted to take Dalton by the shoulders and shake every last piece of information about the bugger out of him.

"Yes, do you know him as well?"

"No," James shook his head and patted Inglot, who had begun to fuss, on the neck to soothe him. "Though I've read much of his work, I'm fascinated by the subject."

"Really?" Dalton raised a bemused eyebrow. "I can't say I feel the same way. Will you be attending his lecture this afternoon? He sent me an invitation, though I can't make it—prior engagements, I'm afraid."

"I hadn't heard he was giving one," James replied slowly, his eyes narrowing thoughtfully. A lecture would be the perfect place to observe this Mr Jackson and see what his competition looked like.

"Lesser known larvae and where to find them, or something along those lines," Dalton supplied and helpfully gave James the time and address where it was to be held. With a few short words of goodbye the men parted ways and James guided Inglot in the direction of his Mayfair home, so that he could change and then go and see what all the fuss was about Alastair Jackson.

The room in Bloomsbury where Jackson was holding his lecture rather reminded James of the schoolrooms in Eton. Rows of seats faced a dusty chalkboard and as he quietly snuck in, a few minutes after the lecture had begun, he had an overwhelming sense of dejavous. He had always been late for lessons when he was a schoolboy—too busy on the rugby pitch— which had earned him more than one lashing. Silently James took a seat in the back row, scanning the room for Jane. He spotted her at the front, resplendent in a dress of forest green, which made her brown hair appear almost auburn. Beside her, wearing the most ridiculous straw bonnet that obscured half the room's view of the chalkboard was Jane's companion, Belinda.

The room was packed with solemn men, who were studiously taking notes of what the speaker was saying. James had been so transfixed by the sight of Jane, that he had momentarily forgotten why he was there.

So you're my competition, he thought sourly as he gave Alastair Jackson the once over. He was a tall man, painfully thin with a long, serious face and glasses perched on the end of his equally long nose. His clothes were dowdy and his voice, when he spoke, had a slight nasally whine. James despised him on the spot. He was exactly the type of pompous git that had picked on him at Eton for being more inclined toward sports than academics; true, once he had grown a few inches in his final years he had had his revenge, but the insults still rankled.

"The most fascinating aspect of the spotted, jungle larvae is how they copulate," Jackson said as James turned his attention to him, rushing over to an easel in the corner of the room, where he placed a large diagram of what Lord

Payne presumed were two copulating larvae. James felt his stomach heave slightly at the sight, though his fellow students began to murmur with excitement and scribble furiously on the pages before them.

"The females then go on to lay their eggs on a host plant, as you can see." Jackson replaced the diagram of the copulating larvae with a less offensive diagram of small, oval eggs and James heaved a sigh of relief. If this was as romantic as Jane's ornithologist got, then there wasn't much in the way of competition. He stole a glance at his fiance, certain that her face would be green with nausea but instead he saw that she was radiant, leaning excitedly forward with her elbows on the table before her.

Oh.

He felt a stab of acute jealousy; he had never known Jane to seem in anyway excited in his company. She usually wore an expression that indicated she was exercising every ounce of patience she possessed to simply be in his presence. He refrained from heaving a self piteous sigh and instead concentrated on the rest of Jackson's lecture which, much to his delight, included a short retelling of the poisonous bite he had received in South America and the three toes that he had to have amputated as a result.

"Bravo,' James called loudly and clapped as the fussy academic finally finished speaking. A multitude of heads turned in his direction, scandalised by the outburst, Jane's included. Her face wore a look of what could only be described as abject horror at his presence. James felt himself bristle under her censure; he was her betrothed, he had every right to be there. It was his duty to protect her and a room full of men was hardly the safest place for two young women to be seen alone. Self righteousness filled him at her reaction and every ounce of sense he might have possessed left him as a result.

The crowd began to trickle out of the room, a few men staying to speak with Mr Jackson whose chest was puffed out, filled with importance. James made his way to the front of the room, to Jane, who seemed to be waiting for everyone to leave before she approached her old paramour.

"What are you doing here?" she hissed crossly, whilst Miss Bowstock gave him a cheery wave.

"Indulging my long held secret passion for larvae," James retorted, equally as irritable as his fiance. "And you? What are you doing out unescorted? It's unseemly for a lady of your rank to attend such events with only Miss Bowstock to accompany you."

He hadn't meant to sound so grumpy and high-handed, but he had ended up doing so despite his best intentions. He saw Jane visibly bristle at his tone, but before he could feel any remorse he spotted Jackson making his way toward them and instead became filled with rage.

"Jane," Jackson said in his nasally tone, "I'm so glad that you came —and you brought friends I see."

Mr Jackson looked pointedly at James and Miss Bowstock, waiting for Jane to introduce them.

"Pleased to meet you, old fellow," James stuck his hand out to take Jackson's in a bone crushing grip, " I am Lord Payne, Jane's betrothed."

"Ah," two bushy eyebrows were raised to heaven in disbelief.

"And this is my companion Miss Belinda Bowstock," Jane interjected, flashing James a warning glance. "It is so lovely to see you again Alastair, after all this time. I am so looking forward to hear of your adventures."

"We both are," James stated, entwining his hand with Jane's. It was with some relief that he noted that she did not yank it away in outrage, humiliating him there and then, though she did squeeze his fingers in a vice-like grip that he was certain would bruise tomorrow.

"Well," Alastair cleared his throat awkwardly, "This is a turn up for the books. I had not realised that you were engaged Jane—and to such a man as Lord Payne. You must feel honoured."

"It is I who is honoured," James corrected him, thinking it was a strange way for Jackson to address the woman he supposedly loved. Jackson should have been threatening James with all kinds of violence for stealing his sweetheart away, but instead he was praising James at the expense of Jane. It was rather bewildering.

"Yes," Jackson cleared his throat again, "It has been wonderful to see you Jane. We must speak again soon. If you'll excuse me, I am expected elsewhere."

The ornithologist hurried from the room, leaving his lecture notes and diagrams behind. James was prone to believe that the elsewhere that Jackson was expected to be was entirely fictitious, though he did not have the opportunity to share this opinion with Jane before she rounded on him angrily.

"What on earth was that?" she questioned, prodding him sharply in the chest with the finger of the hand that she had pulled from his grip.

"What was what?" James huffed. Miss Bowstock mercifully realised that she was caught in the middle of a lover's quarrel and had wandered over to the easel to inspect the hideous diagrams at close quarters with feigned, if exaggerated, interest.

"Don't play stupid with me," Jane hissed. She was truly angry, her cheeks flushed with annoyance, her mouth full and pouting. James knew it wasn't the appropriate time to say it, but he had never seen her look so beautiful.

"You went out of your way to ruin my reunion with Alastair," she continued, "And I can only assume that it's because you want this ridiculous false engagement to go on for as long as suits you. Well, I won't stand to be treated like that Lord Payne. I have enough people in my life who bully me for their own amusement, I won't stand it from you too."

Jane lifted the hem of her skirts and beckoned for Belinda

to follow her, before stalking out the door with her nose stuck in the air. Her blonde haired companion gave James and apologetic smile from under her ridiculous straw bonnet and hastily scurried out after her mistress. James stayed rooted to the spot, guilt flooding his veins and rendering him paralysed. Was he really treating Jane in the same manner as her brother and the awful Viscountess? He knew that his manner had been sparked by a possessiveness and jealousy, though Jane who was not privy to such information, thought him simply selfish, another character in her life who used her for their own self serving whims.

Oh dear, he thought, donning his hat and taking his leave of the shabby brownstone house. Inglot was tethered to the railings of the small square opposite, patiently waiting for his master to return. Once in the saddle, James suddenly decided that he would not return to his own rooms, to wallow in self pity, but instead would visit with someone whose advice he could use.

"For goodness sake, whatever you do, don't tell mother."

Lady Caroline did not look up from the canvas that she was sloshing liberally with paint as she spoke to her brother, seemingly absorbed by her rather dubious artistic creation.

"I know you think me an idiot, Caro," James huffed, feeling like a twelve-year old boy in his sister's presence, as he always did, "But please credit me with some modicum of sense."

"I don't think you an idiot," Caroline finally turned to look at him, her eyes soft with affection. "Though I do wish you would think before you acted —it would save you an awful lot of bother. Come, sit down and tell me everything."

James took a seat on the overstuffed chaise which

dominated the sun-room that his sister used as a studio and, over steaming cups of spiced tea, told her everything. How he had bribed Jane into agreeing to be his fake fiancé, how he had wanted to save her from an uncertain future at the hands of her sister in law and, finally, how he had come to realise that Jane was, in fact, the only woman he could imagine spending his life with.

"Well that's a relief," Caroline heaved a sigh, as his sorry tale came to an end.

"How so?" James questioned, placing his delicate china cup on the table.

"Well," Caroline gave a graceful shrug, her green silk kimono rippling like the sea. "It was patently obvious to all of us that you had coerced Miss Deveraux into agreeing to marry you, but what none of us could figure out was how."

"And who is us?" James asked, slightly affronted that his master plan had been picked apart so easily.

"Well Father, obviously," Caroline answered, a smile tugging at the corner of her lips. James could see that she was trying to suppress a smug grin, for which he was grateful. His battered pride couldn't possibly take another beating. "Giles hazarded a guess after your engagement dinner and Mother —bless her soul— hasn't confessed to anyone that she thinks it's all a ruse, but it's obvious that she does."

"How do you know?"

"Because she's like a woman with a bee in her bonnet, trying to organise the wedding before either of you get a chance to back out. She keeps referring to poor Jane as The Horse Most Likely to Bolt —I think she's forgotten her actual name. You can't blame her, she's just so excited that you've finally brought someone respectable home."

"Oh," James was flummoxed by this information, taken aback by all that Caroline knew. Older sisters were sources of infinite, innate wisdom; the type of wisdom that men could only aspire to a fraction of.

"And now here you are," Caroline finished, "Hoisted by your own petard."

"In boxing they say every man has a plan until he gets punched in the face," James offered, more comfortable with sporting analogies.

"So your nose has been broken by love, little brother, whatever shall we do?" Caroline mused, silent for a few moments as she contemplated her brother's fate.

"All I want is for Jane to be happy, no matter what happens," James said firmly, the guilt at how he had treated her earlier still niggling at his conscience. "Even if it means that she ends up with Jackson, rather than me."

"How noble," Caroline quirked an eyebrow, "You must be in love if you'd put her happiness before her own."

"Well, I am a man Caro," James blushed, "I want to win her hand, but I want to know that I've won it completely —and I know I'm not the most objective observer, but…"

"But what?"

"There's just something that doesn't sit right with me about that Jackson fellow," James grumbled, slightly shamefaced. The man had outright insulted Jane before and yet she had not seemed to mind; perhaps years of suffering at her brother's dismissive hand had inured her to insults. The two siblings fell into thoughtful silence, the only sound in the room being the gentle tattoo of summer rain on the glass roof.

"Leave it to me, James dear," Caroline finally said, "I shall figure out a way for you to win dear Jane's heart."

11 CHAPTER ELEVEN

"I don't see why you had to bring that silly nitwit with you," Emily hissed to Jane as they traipsed up the sweeping steps of Hawkfield Manor. She was referring to Belinda, who tailed the trio of Julian, Emily and Jane as they walked to the door, her mouth open in wonder at the splendour of the house. Jane did not blame her for being impressed; Hawkfield manor was a huge, imposing building; she had counted fifteen bay windows as the carriage had rounded the drive, before giving up completely.

"You were the one who insisted that I needed a companion," Jane whispered back, in annoyance "You can't complain that she's here, when it's entirely your own doing. Besides, Belinda will keep me company for the weekend, leaving you and Julian to do as you please."

The quartet had been invited by the Duke and Duchess of Hawkfield for a weekend house-party at Hawkfield Manor, their sprawling estate in Sussex. Jane had initially been loathe to go, fearing that it was all a ruse and that she would find herself frog-marched down the aisle of a chapel by the Duchess, but Caroline had assured her that would not be the case.

"It's a chance for everyone to relax for a few days, away

from the stuffiness of London. Giles has invited some friends; Harry Dalton and a man he travelled with from South America, whose name I can't recall. He studies something funny, insects, I think —but I'm sure he's nice if he's friends with Harry."

Jane had immediately guessed that who Lady Caroline was speaking of was Alastair. Instantly her attitude to the party changed and she had travelled down from London, buoyant at the the thought of perhaps having some alone time with him. She hoped that the Duchess would not try to engineer any alone time between her and Lord Payne, however. Their limited interactions since the disastrous encounter at Alastair's lecture had been strained; though Lord Payne had tried to redeem himself by being overly solicitous and treating her as though she were made of glass. The way that he had acted before, however, still hurt slightly. Jane had always found Lord Payne's company uplifting, he was quick with a compliment and despite his rakish reputation had always treated her with the utmost kindness. She supposed that what he possessed was an inherent sense of chivalry towards every woman, regardless of her status as a beauty.

Lady Caroline and Giles Bastion were there to greet them, the former engulfing Jane in a warm embrace as she said hello.

"How was the journey?" Caroline enquired solicitously, as she led the way into the vast entrance hall of the house. Even Emily was open mouthed with wonder as the group took in the sheer grandeur of the vast hall. The ceiling appeared to be miles above their heads, supported by a dozen white marble columns which led the way to a sweeping, bifurcated staircase.

"Arduous," Emily complained, her face slightly green. Jane cast her sister in law a worried glance, she had been quiet for the whole of the journey down, not even bothering to be snide when the opportunity arose, and now that she could see her properly she saw that the Viscountess looked quite shaken after all the travel.

"I shall have Mrs Hughes take you directly to your room, you poor thing," Caroline said gamely and directed the rotund housekeeper to take Lord and Lady Jarvis upstairs.

"Mother and Father will likely arrive by the evening," Caroline continued, once she was alone with Jane and Belinda, "And James should arrive shortly. He decided to ride down with the Marquess - he does hate to be confined for too long."

"The Marquess?" Jane asked politely, wishing that Caroline would tell her if Alastair had arrived yet.

"Of Falconbridge," Caroline smiled, "Lord Delaney has been friends with James for eons. It's wonderful that he's agreed to take his head out of his books for a weekend — he's one of the only men who can beat James at a game of cricket."

Unlike Jane, Caroline had not noticed the change that came over Belinda at the mention of Lord Delaney's name. The girl had managed to both blush and turn a ghostly shade of white at the same time, it was quite a remarkable feat. The memory of Belinda having fleetingly mentioned an encounter with the Marquess after her lecture, came to Jane. In all the excitement and confusion of her sudden engagement to Lord Payne she had completely forgotten about it; though seeing Belinda pluck at her dress with a nervous agitation, made Jane resolve to find out what exactly had happened between the two.

"Oh, look," Giles, who unlike his wife was a man of few words, spoke for the first time, startling Jane. He was such a quiet man that she had almost forgotten that he was there. "Here comes James now."

Jane followed Lady Caroline and her husband to the open door and joined them at the top of the sweeping, granite steps, where they waited for Lord Payne and the Marquess to reach the top of the driveway.

"This is quite the welcome party," James called happily as

he dismounted his stallion, passing the reins to a footman who had leapt to attention at the sight of Hawkfield's heir. Lord Payne was in excellent spirits after the journey, a grin almost splitting his face in two. He looked most dashing, Jane conceded, his hair tousled, his coat abandoned in favour of a shirt, which was rolled up at the sleeves, revealing sinewy, muscular forearms that left Jane feeling a little queer. He was so masculine, his shoulders broad, his body hard and athletic —she had become so used to him that it was a part of him she overlooked, though seeing him now, she was at a loss as to how she had become immune to her fiance's rugged handsomeness.

"It is lovely to see you Lord Payne," she finally said, her voice an octave higher than usual, "And you Lord Delaney."

"Miss Deveraux," the Marquess gave a curt bow. Unlike his companion Lord Delaney looked completely unruffled by the ride to Hawkfield Hall. His clothes were immaculate, as though he had just been dressed by a fastidious valet and there was not a hair out of place on his head. Like James he was tall, but unlike James his manner was cool, almost glacial.

Lady Caroline fussed about the new arrivals and once everyone was collected together in the hall, she arranged for Mrs Hughes, who had returned, to show Jane and Belinda to their suite of rooms.

"Put Miss Bowstock in the lavender room," she instructed the housekeeper, then turned, her fine, porcelain features a picture of confusion. "Where has she gone?"

"I'm here," Belinda squeaked, her face pink, as she stepped out from behind one of the marble pillars. She kept her eyes to the floor as she made her way over to Jane, apparently too afraid to look up. Jane could understand why, for the seemingly unflappable Marquess of Falconbridge had suddenly turned scarlet at the sight of the blonde haired young lady.

"Follow me," Jane whispered to her flustered companion,

slipping her arm through the crook of Belinda's elbow, "I'll help you to our rooms - and when we get there you are going to have to do some explaining."

The guests did not meet again until much later that evening, when a large supper was held to welcome them. Jane arrived at the dinning room feeling much refreshed after a bath and a long nap. The long journey in the carriage had left her sore, even though the Viscount's vehicle was modern and well sprung. It seemed to have affected the Viscountess as well, for Julian stated, with a little annoyance in his tone, that Emily would not make it down for the meal.

"Is she alright?" Jane whispered, worried for the younger woman, who was usually loathe to miss a chance to socialise.

"She's fine," Julian shrugged, sipping deeply on the glass of wine he held in his hand, "She's just being childish, nothing more."

Goodness, Jane started, for she had never heard Julian speak of his new bride with anything other than slavish devotion in his voice. She hoped that whatever was brewing between the pair blew over quickly, for though she was not overly fond of Emily she did want her to enjoy her weekend away from town.

The other guests began to trickle in, the Marquess of Falconbridge among them. Jane saw him scan the room, looking for Belinda, though her companion had pleaded a migraine and, like the Viscountess, had decided to stay in her room. Jane glared at the immaculately clad Marquess, who stood aloof at the edge of the room. Belinda had told her that he had given her a mighty dressing down in Montagu House, for touching the ancient Roman urns, and that was the source of the tension between the two. Honestly, what a pompous, arrogant man the Marquess was.

The door opened and Jane's heart leapt with excitement as Alastair and Harry Dalton entered the room. Alastair was dressed in what Jane knew to be his best attire, an old-fashioned suit coat over dark breeches. She couldn't help but compare him to the James, whose clothes were always the height of fashion, but felt a stab of guilt at this treacherous thought.

Of course James wears nicer clothes, she chided herself, he's next in line to be a Ducal title for heaven's sake! Alastair was not a wealthy, he had given his life over to his studies and that in itself was a hundred times more admirable than a wardrobe from Saville Row.

"Miss Deveraux," Harry Dalton gave a wide smile and walked over to where she stood, "I believe you know Mr Jackson."

"Hello Mr Dalton," Jane said, "I do of course know Mr Jackson. Gentlemen allow me to introduce my brother, Lord Deveraux, Viscount Jarvis."

The men exchanged handshakes before Julian wandered off to find a servant to refill his glass. Jane nibbled her lip nervously; if he continued to drink at the same pace, he'd be well in his cups before the first course was served.

"Did you travel down together?" Jane enquired, directing her question to Alastair, who for some reason was staring at the other side of the room.

"Indeed, we did," Harry Dalton said, after it became clear that his companion was not going to answer Jane. "It was kind of Lady Caroline to invite us. The Duke has been generous enough to sponsor so many of my trips, I feel greedy having him feed me as well when I return."

"I am sure he would not sponsor you Mr Dalton if he did not believe that your explorations were mere fanciful adventures."

"I do acquire him a few treasures along my way," Dalton conceded, with a charming smile. "Alastair is hoping that the Duke might take an interest in his own studies, and perhaps fund his return to South America."

"So soon?" Jane gasped; surely he would not leave her again, when they had barely had a moment together.

"There is very little to keep me in England," Alastair responded, finally meeting her eyes with a cool, dismissive glance.

Before Jane could respond that she was reason enough to stay, the Duke and Duchess arrived and the guests were seated at the table. Throughout the first course she kept glancing across at Alastair, hoping to catch his eye, but he stared resolutely at his plate, obviously wishing to avoid her.

"Have you visited Hawkfield before Miss Deveraux?" the Marquess, who was seated to her right, asked politely.

"Never," she shook her head as she took a small bite of the broiled chicken on her plate, "And you, my Lord?"

"Quite a bit during my childhood," Falconbridge responded easily, "Though I have spent much time abroad and have not visited in many years. It is nice to return and even nicer to see that Payne has finally settled down."

The last sentence was delivered in a dry tone and Jane could see that the Marquess was resisting rolling his eyes. They were quite opposite, Lord Payne and he. Where James radiated energy and good humour, the Marquess was cool and aloof. Everything about him seemed highly controlled —which made Belinda's tale of him having lost his temper with her quite unbelievable. The man seemed completely unflappable.

As the third course was served Jane looked up and caught Lord Payne gazing at her with an expression that was akin to longing. She felt her stomach flip as she registered the gentle warmth in his eyes. Don't be ridiculous, she thought with annoyance, it's not longing, it's probably just indigestion. Though as platters of cheese and grapes were set down before the assembled guests, signalling the end of the meal, she caught him gazing at her again. Perhaps he's drunk, she thought, as she nibbled on some cheddar. Though she quickly placed the cheese back on her plate, for her appetite had disappeared at the strange feeling that bloomed in her stomach each time she caught Lord Payne's eye.

Indigestion, she repeated firmly, wishing she believed herself.

12 CHAPTER TWELVE

"Thus far, sister dear, your plan for Jane to fall helplessly in love with me has fallen flat on its face," James grumbled. He and Caroline were walking side by side, leading the guests on an excursion through the vast grounds of the Hawkfield estate. The day was unusually warm for early summer, and Caroline had decided that an impromptu picnic by the lake would be much preferable to a day of hunting for the men and shopping in the village for the ladies.

"Well that's because you're walking beside me and not your intended," Caroline replied easily, "How is she supposed to submit to your charms, when you're wasting them on me? Though if grumbling is the height of witty banter you can offer poor Jane, then I don't blame her for choosing to walk alongside Mr Jackson."

James bristled with annoyance at the mention of the wretched man's name. At the beginning of the walk Jackson had lagged behind the group, and James had been startled to see that Jane had adopted the same pace. The group was nearly at the lake and the pair had been deep in conversation for the past twenty minutes, oblivious to all around them.

"Dalton told Giles that Mr Jackson is hoping father will sponsor him to go back on his trip to the South Americas," Caroline confided in a whisper, throwing a coy glance over her shoulder at the ornithologist. "If you drop a word in father's ear, I'm sure he'll agree to it and then Jane will be free of him."

"I don't want to win by duplicitous means, Caro," James grumbled, "I want Jane to give me her heart because she loves me, not because her first choice disappeared to chase worms around a jungle."

Caroline sighed and James knew it was because she thought that he was being overly competitive —which he was. He loved to win, because winning meant that he was the best. When it came to Jane he wanted her to choose him because in her eyes he was the best option—the only option.

"Here we are," he called, as the group rounded the corner. Before them the ground sloped downward, leading to a calm, freshwater lake which was filled with trout. The servants had laid out the picnic and a few footmen were standing discreetly by the blankets, in case they were needed.

"Such a beautiful view," James heard Miss Bowstock exclaim, "If only I had brought my sketchpad."

She might have forgotten her drawing pencils, but Miss Bowstock had remembered her King Charles Cavalier who, upon sniffing the picnic went tearing across the grass, with the hapless Belinda running behind him, calling for him to stop.

"Oh, dear," Jane cried, "She'll lose her bonnet running like that."

"That would hardly be a tragedy," Lord Delaney drawled.

James stifled a snort, for the Marquess was quite right; it

truly was the most hideous hat. The group watched in awe as Jane's prediction came true and Miss Bowstock's bonnet went flying off her head toward the lake. The young woman halted in her tracks, her head swivelling toward the dog, who was intent on reaching the picnic and her hat, which was now floating on the surface of the lake. She obviously decided that lunch was more important, for she tore after the dog again, whilst the Marquess heaved a sigh and headed in the direction of the lake.

"Oh, dear," James heard Jane whisper again, as she watched the Marquess step into the shallow water. "He'll ruin his boots."

"Unlikely," James gave her a smile, "They're leather, and I have known Delaney for long enough to know that he'd never risk ruining a pair of good boots."

This seemed to mollify Jane, who turned and gave him a smile. It was like standing directly in the sun's rays, James thought, returning her grin with one of his own.

"My dear, the servants have been up all morning preparing this luncheon," he stated grandly, tucking her arm into the crook of his, "And I don't mean to pressure you, but there are several footmen taking notes for the cook on if the future Duchess of Hawkfield enjoyed the meal."

"Really?" Jane whipped her head around to stare suspiciously at the innocent footmen.

"Not really," James laughed, "Though they will notice if you eat nothing. Then they will tell cook, who is French and quite temperamental. He will have a minor fit and threaten to quit. Then none of us shall eat for the rest of the weekend."

"I fear the duties of a Duchess would be too much for me," Jane laughed, "Thank goodness I will never have to shoulder the burden."

"I don't know," James replied lightly, though for him his response felt anything but light, "I feel you'd do an admirable job as Duchess."

A part of him wanted to make a joke to ease the

uncertainty that crossed Jane's face at his serious tone, though he refrained. He wanted her to sense how serious his intentions toward her had become.

"Well then I shall have to try a little of everything, my Lord," she finally responded gamely, squaring her shoulders as though going into battle and not to a picnic.

"I've told you to call me James," James halted their stride, turning to gaze down at her. "I like the sound of my name coming from your lips. I have never heard a sweeter sound."

"Really, my Lord, you are being ridiculous."

James relished at the blush which slowly began to stain Jane's cheeks, she was completely, totally and utterly charming when she was flustered. It made a lovely change to the usual calm, steady way that she dealt with him. A wicked thought, that he would like to tease her until the blush crept all the way down to her decolletage, sprang to mind —though he pushed it reluctantly away. There would be plenty of time for that later, when they were wed.

"Here come the two love-birds," Caroline called, as he and Jane joined the group by the blankets which had been laid under the shade of a copse of ancient oaks. "You nearly missed the food, you were too busy making cow eyes at each other."

"I was not making cow eyes," Jane looked startled at the accusation, "Lord Payne and I were merely discussing…"

She trailed off, and James had the pleasure of watching her grapple for something to say.

"…Jane's future responsibilities as Duchess," James supplied, and she gave him a grateful glance.

"Oh they'll be manifold and utterly tedious," Caroline said cheerfully, beckoning the pair to sit down on the blankets, "Though I'm sure James will make it up to you in other ways."

This entendre raised a chuckle from her husband and James, though grateful to his sister, felt slightly nauseated as the pair shared a secret smile.

"Allow me to serve you," he whispered in Jane's ear, rising lightly to his feet and fetching two plates, which he piled high with strawberries, cold meats and bread. When he returned, much to his annoyance, he found Miss Bowstock seated beside Jane, so close that she was practically sitting in her lap.

"My Lord," she smiled at him, and continued to smile inanely, her head turned at an awkward angle. James spotted the Marquess directly behind her shoulder, glowering at her, and guessed that this was why Miss Bowstock was acting so strangely.

"I apologise Miss Bowstock, I did not fetch you a plate," James stated, feeling as though he had walked into a play halfway through. What on earth was going on between Jane's companion and Delaney? He hadn't known that the two were even acquainted and yet here Delaney was, glaring daggers at him for daring to speak to Belinda.

"I shall fetch Miss Bowstock a plate," the Marquess said gruffly, standing to reveal that his breeches were soaked to the knee and that his boots were utterly ruined. The sorry looking bonnet that he had rescued sat beside Belinda on the blanket, it's ribbons soiled with muddy lake water.

"Oh dear," she whispered to the the pair, once the Marquess was out of earshot, "I fear that Lord Delaney is a trifle upset over his boots —though I did not ask him to wade into the lake. He was quite right when he said that the bonnet was hideous, I only wear it because I don't own any others."

"Hush Belinda," Jane reached out and gave the girl's hand a squeeze, "Don't pay any attention to the Marquess, I won't let him upset you."

Indeed Jane looked rather fierce and protective; James truly believed that she would go into battle to protect her friend's feelings. If only she would do the same for herself.

"Jane, dearest," the Viscountess called, her high voice carrying clearly, "Fix your bonnet, I can see the freckles on your nose from all the way over here."

Jane said nothing in reply, merely pulled at the ribbons of her bonnet to show she had been listening.

"I don't know why you let her speak to you that way," James whispered, his hand reaching out of its own volition to push the brim of Jane's hat back, so he could better see her eyes. Which at that moment were filled with confusion at his overly familiar gesture.

"What do you mean?" she asked in confusion. The re-arrival of the Marquess meant that James could not further question Jane on why she allowed her brother and his wife to bully her so. The Marquess handed Belinda a plate piled high with food, though the poor girl looked as though she were about to cast up her accounts as she took it from him. That would render his boots thoroughly ruined, James thought with wry amusement.

The guests fell silent as they began to tuck into their lunch, the only sounds being the occasional exclamation on how delicious the food was. After they had eaten, Harry Dalton suggested a game of cricket.

"We're about eighteen men short for a proper game," James grinned, though he readily stood up to play. The ladies remained seated, lounging on their blankets as they watched the men assemble into two teams of two, with Jackson opting to play the umpire.

It was good fun and James became so absorbed in the process that he had not noticed that the ladies had wandered to the lake's edge, until a startled cry went up. He turned to see Jane picking herself up from the reeds, her dress sodden up to the knees.

"Jane," he called, abandoning the game altogether and rushing to her side.

"Honestly, look at you. You've ruined your new dress and embarrassed yourself in the process."

The Viscountess stood beside her sister-in-law, offering no help but a tirade of insults as Jane clambered to the shore.

"Are you alright?" James asked, taking Jane's arm and turning her toward him. He could see that her bottom lip was trembling and in her eyes he could see tears forming.

"Come," he said, reaching out and hauling her up into his arms, "I'll have to get you back to the house before you catch a chill."

Ignoring her protests he lifted her up, cradling her to his chest as he made his way back toward the house.

"Honestly, Lord Payne, I am quite capable of walking," she protested, struggling slightly against his iron grip.

"You may have twisted an ankle," he reasoned, as they walked through the door of Hawkfield House, the footmen staring in shock at the sight of them.

"I think I would know if I had twisted my ankle," Jane protested, though she had stopped struggling and allowed him to carry her up the two flights of stairs to her suite of rooms.

Once outside the door James hesitated; he had rather enjoyed the feel of holding Jane in his arms, but even he knew that propriety dictated he should not cross the threshold of her bedroom door. If he did he knew that the temptation to fling her on to the bed and ravish her with kisses would be far too strong to overcome.

"You may leave me here, my Lord, thank you," Jane said primly, reaching a hand out to the door frame to steady herself as she escaped his grip.

"I have told you to call me James, have I not?"

His words came out as a throaty whisper and as Jane turned to look at him quizzically, James leaned forward and captured her open lips with his own. It was like no kiss he had ever known; Jane was so sweet and innocent, meeting his demanding lips with an innocent hesitation that tore at his heart.

"Jane," he whispered, his hands reaching out to tangle themselves through her thick, silky tresses. She responded with a soft moan of longing, which seemed to take her by surprise.

"Oh, we shouldn't," she whispered in a half hearted protest, but fell silent as James claimed her mouth with his again. As the kiss deepened she became more confident, allowing him to nibble on her bottom lip and slip his tongue slowly inside the soft recesses of her mouth.

"Jane," he groaned, feeling thoroughly undone by her. He had kissed courtesans, actresses, opera singers and many of the *demi monde* seductresses —but this was unlike anything he had ever known. This was wild, this was passionate...this was love.

"Oh, I'm sorry!"

They had been so caught up in their embrace that they had failed to hear the sound of footsteps approaching. Miss Bowstock, battered bonnet in hand, stood a few feet away, her face bright red with embarrassment.

"I came to see if Jane was alright," she stated, glancing at Jane nervously, "I'll go—"

"No," Jane called, almost desperately, her expression nervous. She could not look James in the eye and he cursed the passion which had caused him to almost ravish her in the hallway.

"Please help Miss Deveraux change before she catches a chill," James said, in as commanding a voice as he could muster. With a curt bow to Jane, who still looked charmingly dishevelled, he hurried away down the corridor. A chill, what a ridiculous thought, there was no way either of them was at risk of feeling cold after their heated embrace. Even better, James thought smugly, Jane Deveraux had responded to his passion with excitement that matched his own. He was still in the race for her heart and if he played his cards right, he might yet win.

13 CHAPTER THIRTEEN

Jane stood at the window of her bedroom, gazing out into the garden below. She took no notice of the rose garden which bloomed below her, or the landscaped lawns beyond, for her mind had wandered from the present and was fixed on those few minutes with James. He had kissed her! Lord Payne had kissed her. It had been delicious, it had been exciting, it had been utterly and thoroughly confusing.

Jane had never been kissed before, excepting one perfunctory peck on the lips from Alastair, which had filled her dreams for years. The idea that she had found that cold kiss passionate, now made her laugh. For Lord Payne had shown her what true passion was; it was barely restrained, a heady rush of emotions and a million soft sensations.

She touched her lips, which she was sure must be swollen, and smiled. Then she frowned, for she had no idea why she was smiling. Why had Lord Payne kissed her? He was not in love in with her, that much she knew. He was also not such a rake that he would try to steal liberties from her, simply because he could. Of that, Jane was certain.

It was terribly confusing and the only person she could ask about it was Belinda, who had dreamily declared that Lord Payne must be harbouring a secret desire for his fake fiance.

Which was balderdash.

She was Plain Jane, Queen of a thousand books and endless facts and figures. She wore spectacles, she fussed and was painfully shy; she did not dance, sing and act charmingly in public like Payne's other lovers.

She twisted the ring on her finger nervously, as she contemplated what had happened. Her mind was naturally scientific and she believed that nothing happened without just cause —excepting this. This kiss had rendered her mind unable to reason the why, where or how —but, oh, how lovely it had felt.

A knock on the door startled her from her reverie and without waiting for a reply the Viscountess Jarvis let herself into the room.

"There you are Jane," Emily sighed, sounding annoyed, as if Jane had been hiding in some hidden cupboard and not her bed-chambers.

"Emily," Jane tried to inject a small bit of warmth into her voice at the sight of her sister-in-law. The young woman still looked pale, her lips a startling red against her alabaster skin. She truly did look ill, Julian was wrong to have declared her simply childish.

"Have you recovered from your impromptu swim?" Emily asked, moving restlessly around the room, examining paintings and picking up ornaments as she went.

"Quite," Jane said delicately. An apology had been on the tip of her lips, though she hesitated to offer it. Lady Caroline had called to her room to check on her well being and when Jane had apologised for making a spectacle of herself, the older woman had brushed it away.

"It was an accident, don't say sorry, I'm just glad you're unhurt."

It had been a revelation of sorts to Jane, who felt like she had spent a lifetime saying sorry for every minor discretion she had made. The Fairweather's were warm and caring, where Julian had always been cruel and unpleasant.

"I am glad," Emily said, her back turned to Jane as she read the spine of the book Jane had brought with her to read before bed. "A History of Hieroglyphics?"

"Giles mentioned that it was fascinating, I believe it is the Marquess' field of study."

"Riveting," Jane could hear the sarcasm in Emily's voice. The young woman turned as though to leave and then stumbled, her face deathly white.

"Emily," Jane cried, rushing forward to catch the girl by the elbows and helping her to the bed. "Whatever's the matter?"

To Jane's shock, tears began to well in Emily's cornflower blue eyes.

"I-I-," she stuttered, heaving sobs rendering her almost indecipherable. "I am increasing."

"Why, Emily, that's wonderful news!" Jane declared, excited by the prospect of a little niece or nephew to spoil. This only made Emily's sobbing worse however and the young woman shook her head stubbornly at Jane's words.

"It's awful," she whispered, her face achingly young looking and tear-stained. "I feel ill all day long, I can't keep any food down and I—and I—"

Jane waited for the Viscountess to finish the bout of sobbing that wracked her tiny frame again.

"I am afraid of dying."

"Of dying?" Jane exclaimed, she had not been expecting

that. "Don't be silly Emily, you won't die in child-birth. Julian will make sure that you have the best physicians in all of England attending to you."

"That's what he said," Emily howled in response, "He told me I was being silly and childish. But women do die, Jane, like Sophie…"

"Who was Sophie?" Jane questioned, her brow furrowed. She had never heard the name mentioned in her life.

"She was my sister in law," Emily sniffed, taking the hankie that Jane proffered and blowing her nose. "She married my brother five years ago and we were the greatest of friends. Then she became with child and then…"

Emily's voice trailed to nothing and Jane filled in the blanks herself. Poor Sophie, to have died so young and poor Emily, who had obviously loved her.

"Well, I won't let you die," Jane said firmly, hoping that this would soothe the poor Viscountess.

"You won't?" Emily looked at her hopefully and Jane felt a stab of pity for the girl, who really was no more than a child.

"I won't," she repeated, drawing Emily into a warm hug. "And I will have words with my brother about how he has treated you. A woman who is increasing should not be upset in any way. If he's not grovelling on his hands and knees by the end of today, then I'll eat Belinda's hat."

"It really is a hideous bonnet," Emily said with a watery smile.

"With any luck the next time it might fall into a pile of cow dung and become completely irreparable," Jane said with a grin. What a day it had been, between Lord Payne and the Viscountess —who knew what other secret sides people were hiding?

Later that evening, after supper the guests gathered in the drawing room for music and games. Belinda revealed a hitherto hidden talent for the piano forte. She regaled the guests with numerous songs, until the Marquess of Falconbridge came to stand beside her and she suddenly lost her place.

"Oh, dear," she stuttered, pushing back the chair and standing up, "I've run out of songs…"

She scurried back to the sofa where Jane sat and point blank refused to stand up again, despite the Duchess of Hawkfield's pleading and Falconbridge's glowering expression.

"Honestly, child, I have never heard a voice so pure. Who taught you how to sing?"

"My mother," Belinda answered quietly, her face turning to Jane with a pleading look. Sensing that her companion did not wish to discuss her tragic family history, Jane changed the topic, suggesting a game of charades.

"Too boring," Julian called from the corner of the room that he had settled himself in.

"A board game?" Lady Caroline offered, though as it turned out the only game they had was chess, which could not be played by a dozen people at once.

"How about hide and seek?" Lord Payne asked.

"Perfect," Julian slurred, "If you're looking for me, I'll be in the library with your father by the brandy decanter."

"And I am far too old to be playing such childish games," the Duchess declared, beckoning for a maid to follow her as she left the room.

The rest of the guests remained, the men pulling straws to see who would be the seeker, whilst the women laughed and joked among themselves. Jane was glad to see that Emily seemed much brighter, despite Julian's poor show of manners.

"Gah, I knew it would be me," Giles said in his deep baritone as he pulled the shortest straw. "Alright get hiding, you have until the count of twenty."

It was ridiculously childish, but Jane felt a rush of excitement as she fled the room, the others chasing after her. She turned right, down a corridor she had not ventured into and quickly dived in behind the first door she saw. It was a parlour of sorts, cluttered with furniture and bric a brac.

"This is Mrs Hughes private sitting room," a voice said, accompanying the sound of the door opening.

Jane turned, startled that she had been discovered so soon, but relaxed when she saw that it was just Lord Payne.

"You gave me a fright," she whispered in a scolding tone, "I thought you were Giles."

"I'd be frightened to be alone in a room with him too," Payne offered her a roguish smile, that she could not help but return, despite the new onset of nerves at his words. Being alone in a room with the steady, married Giles Bastion would be much preferable in Jane's eyes to her current situation. She was alone with Lord Payne —the man who, just a few hours before, had kissed her most thoroughly.

Her heart began to beat erratically and, as though he could hear it, James held out his hand to take hers. His grip was steady and reassuring as he pulled her against his chest.

"Oh, Jane," he whispered into her hair, inhaling deeply. She could feel the rise and fall of his chest as he breathed in and hear the sound of his heart thumping. Its pace matched the wild pace of her own, she realised, was it possible that Payne was as nervous of her as she was of him?

"I have been longing for a moment alone with you," he said finally, stepping backward so that he could look her in the eye. He was breathtakingly handsome in that moment, his dark blond locks falling into his eyes, a hesitant smile playing around the corners of his lips.

"I do not think we should spend too much time here, my—James," she responded nervously, "It's not proper."

"As we are betrothed we are allowed to bend the rules of propriety, ever so slightly," James replied, his hand reaching out to tuck a stray piece of her hair behind her ear.

"We are not actually betrothed, as you well know," Jane countered, wondering if she had misjudged him terribly. Was he truly a rake who would try to take liberties with her?

"Yes, you keep reminding me of that fact."

His tone was slightly annoyed and Jane, who had spent a lifetime deciphering the nuanced moods of others, glanced at him nervously.

"I only remind you, because you keep forgetting," she countered, wrapping her arms around herself to ward off the chill of the evening.

"That's because I don't want you to be my pretend fiance anymore."

"You wish to end the whole charade?" Jane asked —did he believe his father was now convinced he had changed his ways?

"No, blast it," James sighed, pushing back his hair with an agitated hand. "I want you to be my wife Jane. I want you to stand beside me as the Duchess of Hawkfield, bear my heirs and love me as I love you."

"As you…?"

"I love you."

Never had a declaration of love seemed so filled with pain, Jane thought with alarm. Payne was watching her with anguished eyes and she realised that he was waiting for her response in the same way a condemned man awaited his punishment.

"I-," she said, grappling for something to say. She loved James for his kindness, for his humour, for the way that he brought joy and happiness into her life —but she did not know if she was in love with him. Indeed, she did not believe that he was in love with her, he had probably had a sneaky nip or two of brandy after dinner and decided that after their kiss he was. It would be very like Lord Payne to act in such an impulsive manner. Anger began to build inside her; anger that he could be so callous with her feelings. He could declare himself in love today, only to take it back tomorrow.

"I don't believe you," she whispered, heat flushing her cheeks. "I think you have gotten a silly idea into your head and have decided to ask me to play along. I won't be a part of any more of your charades Lord Payne. When we return to London I shall break the engagement and, perhaps, marry Alastair. He is a steady, reliable—"

The list of Alastair Jackson's many attributes was cut off as Payne took her by the wrist and pulled her against him once more. His lips claimed hers in a hungry, demanding kiss, that left her knees weak and her head dizzy.

"I never want to hear that man's name from your lips again," James growled between searing kisses. His hands roved her body, sending frissons of pleasure through her, and though she knew that they should stop, Jane could not bring herself to bring the embrace to an end. It was the most heady, passionate moment of her life and it would have gone on forever had the door not opened and Giles Bastion burst in.

"There you are -oh!" he called, his voice faltering as he took in who was there and what exactly it was that they were doing.

"Oh, I do apologise," he said discreetly, making to back out of the door he had just come through.

"No, don't," Jane called, seeking to take advantage of his inopportune entrance, "You have found us Mr Bastion, well done. I would love to play another game, but I fear I have come down with a terrible migraine."

Without a backward glance to Lord Payne, who she knew was standing in the spot that she had left him, Jane fled the room, seeking the solace and sanctuary of her bedchamber.

14 CHAPTER FOURTEEN

Well that had gone abysmally, James thought as he took a deep sip on his brandy. After Jane had pleaded a migraine and gone to bed, the other ladies had followed suit, leaving the men to engage in, well, manly pursuits. If drinking brandy and playing five card loo could be considered manly.

James was seated in the mahogany lined library with Giles, Jackson, Falconbridge and Harry Dalton. His father and the Viscount Jarvis had long since drank themselves into a stupor and retired for the night.

"Loo," Dalton called happily through a thick cloud of cheroot smoke.

"Again?" Jackson grumbled, tossing his cards down on the table in disgust at having lost another game to his friend.

"You have the luck of the devil," James commented lightly, throwing his own cards on the table. They were not gambling for large sums and he was not paying much attention to the game, so he did not feel put out by Dalton's success. Indeed, the only person who seemed to be upset was Alastair Jackson; his face had turned red with annoyance and he wore a scowl that could curdle milk.

"Yes, you win every game of cards, win the sponsorship of one of the highest ranking men in England. Is there anything you don't win Dalton?"

"A respite from your moaning,apparently." the explorer retorted to Jackson's grumblings. James tried valiantly to resist chortling, but despite his best efforts a guffaw of amusement escaped him. Jackson's face turned redder and he picked up the cards and began to shuffle them furiously.

"Now, now gentlemen."

Ever the voice of reason, Giles held up a hand to hush the bickering between the trio. He was the only man there who wasn't completely foxed, James realised. Dalton and Jackson were in their cups and he wasn't too far behind. The Marquess, who had been watching the game with a detached interest, had also been drinking steadily since the ladies had disappeared. It seemed every man, bar Giles, was unhappy.

"How goes the search for the missing Egyptian Stone, Falconbridge?" Giles asked in a most blatant attempt to change the subject.

"It doesn't," the Marquess sighed, allowing James to refill his glass with a generous measure of brandy. "I have been waylaid by a family matter. My late wife's cousin died and in his will he appointed me guardian of his daughter, but the girl has all but disappeared. Now, instead of trying to solve the mystery of what happened to the stone once the French surrendered Cairo, I'm searching for my missing ward."

"Any idea where she might be?" James asked, his interest piqued. Falconbridge was notoriously private, to hear him speak of anything that wasn't related to deciphering dead languages was a novelty.

"No," Falconbridge sighed, setting his tumbler down for James to refill, "She seems to have disappeared off the face of the earth. If any of you happen upon a Miss Hestia B. Stockbow, be sure to let me know."

"Shall do," James raised his glass in a toast to the missing ward, "Now - shall we deal again?"

Dalton cut another deck and the men began playing again. A hint of devilry filled James and he kept raising the stake of the buy in, not by astronomical amounts, but enough so that Jackson's face turned a startling shade of puce.

"I'm out," the ornithologist said in disgust, as he lost yet another round.

"Bad luck, old chap," James called, throwing his own cards on the table carelessly.

"That's the only type of luck I seem to have," Jackson replied morosely, "Nothing has gone right since that blasted spider crawled into my boot."

"Amputations are never easy," the Marquess said solemnly. James rather thought that the amputations Delaney had witnessed during the war were slightly more harrowing than Jackson's two lost toes, but he kept silent.

"Yes. Lost my toes. Lost the woman I thought I would marry upon my return..." Jackson gave James a dark look as he finished this statement.

"You didn't lose her," James retorted angrily, "You left her to go hunting for insects. It's your own tough luck that somebody else snapped her up in you absence."

"Indeed," Jackson took his spectacles off and began polishing the lens on his coat sleeve. "Snapped up by someone who was clever enough to realise he wouldn't have to wait for his father to die, in order to become a wealthy man."

"I beg your pardon?"

Had Jackson really just insinuated that he was only marrying Jane for her enormous dowry?

"You heard me," the weedy man responded churlishly, his words slurred from brandy. "There's no other reason a man like you would marry a woman like Jane, if it wasn't for her enormous dowry. You were hardly attracted by her stunning good lucks. Oh, if I had had the foresight to marry her before I left for South America I could still be there, studying-argh!"

Jackson's piteous ode to his lost chance was cut off by James' fist connecting with his jaw. It took the other men, who were all half-drunk, a few moments to react, allowing James the chance to get a few blows in before he was dragged off the awful man. In his drunken state he thought he saw a face, pale and white against the darkness, peering in the doorway, but when he looked again it was gone.

"James, you can't strike your guests," Giles reasoned, as he forcibly restrained his brother in law, "No matter how reprehensible a fellow he is."

"I was merely stating what everybody else has been thinking," Jackson called, wiping his bloody nose.

"That's enough," Harry Dalton cut across, glaring at his friend. "You have insulted Lord Payne's intended, under his own roof no less. You're lucky all he delivered was a blow -he could have called you out for that. We will depart at once for London."

"There's no need to leave so soon, Dalton," Giles soothed, throwing a grateful glance at the Marquess who had grabbed James by the elbow, "It's too late to set off for Town."

"Well, we shall depart at sunrise," the explorer relented, "And I can only hope you will forgive me for bringing Jackson along."

"Actually it was Caroline who insisted he came," Giles said in a loud stage whisper, "I fear I might have to have a word or two with my wife about meddling. Goodnight

Dalton, I shall see you soon. Good night Mr Jackson, it's - ah- been interesting."

Giles placed his body between James and Jackson as the latter stumbled from the room. Once the door had shut firmly behind the pair, a solemn Giles walked over to the table and poured three measures of brandy.

"A toast," he said, raising his glass once he had given the others theirs. "To a most admirable punch. If ever a blighter deserved a crack on the jaw it was Jackson."

"Hear, hear," Falconbridge let go of James' elbow, to lift his glass.

"I shouldn't have hit him," James moaned, ignoring his glass of spirits. Jane would be furious with him when she found out —though he could never tell her of what Jackson had said. To know that the man she thought loved her, saw her as no more than a coin-purse with legs, would be a devastating blow.

"Don't worry about it James," Giles gave a shrug, "He'll be gone in the morning and then you can forget that Alastair Jackson even exists. God knows, I will…"

Except the next morning, when the house awoke, they rose to find that not only had Mr Jackson fled the vicinity, but so had Miss Deveraux.

15 CHAPTER FIFTEEN

"Well aren't you a sight for sore eyes!"

Polly Jenkin's greeting to Jane was delivered in her usual cheerful, Northern accent. Jane thought that perhaps it was the sweetest sound she had ever heard, but then she had been travelling alone in a stage-coach for days. Any sound that wasn't her own tortured thoughts was most welcome.

"Where have you come from then?" Polly asked suspiciously as Jane followed her into the hall, her portmanteau in hand. The flaxen haired woman gave her a quick once over, noting, no doubt, Jane's bedraggled appearance and travel dusty clothes.

"From Sussex," Jane stated, to which Polly gave a snort.

"You look like you've travelled from the seventh circle of hell, lass," she replied, ushering Jane into the kitchen. "Not ruddy Sussex."

Once she was seated at the solid wooden table, Jane allowed herself to relax. The boarding house in St Jarvis had always been her refuge, and even though its proprietress had changed, she still felt safe within its walls. She watched Polly silently, as the woman bustled to and fro as she brewed a pot of tea. Once she had added the requisite milk and sugar, Polly sat down on the seat opposite Jane.

"Tell me what happened lass," she said calmly, then listened as Jane poured out the sorry saga of her engagement to James and what she had overheard in the library.

"That slimy slug," Polly said with a scowl, as Jane finished relating the disparaging things that Alastair had said about her. "Does Lord Payne know that you were eavesdropping?"

"I wasn't eavesdropping," Jane responded, a little aggrieved at the accusation. "I simply overheard."

"Of course..."

Jane knew that Polly was only mollifying her, but she ignored it; she didn't have the energy for an argument.

"Now, I'm not as clever as you," Polly said, after a pause in which both women sipped thoughtfully on their tea. "But from what I'm gathering a good man defended your honour and you repaid him by disappearing in the middle of the night, without a word as to where you were going."

"That's not what happened," Jane gasped, shocked by Polly's directness. "I was humiliated. I told Payne that I could not marry him because of the love that Alastair and I shared. How could I look him in the eye knowing that he knows me to be stupid, love-struck idiot?"

"Do you think Lord Payne would think that of you?" Polly questioned lightly. Jane paused, thinking of all that she knew of James. He was the one person in her life who had always treated her with kindness and respect. He was probably, at that very moment, suffering because her pride had not allowed her to face him.

"I know he would not," Jane relented, fidgeting with the material of her dress. "But I cannot return to London Polly. I cannot face him, nor Julian. He'll be furious with me for vanishing."

"Lud," the Northerner heaved a sigh, "I have never known such an intelligent woman get herself into such a silly scrape. Chin up though, love. Mrs Actrol is in residence and is giving a reading of her latest manuscript later."

Mrs Actrol was an author, who spent a great deal of time at the boarding house. She had been fast friends with the previous proprietress, Mrs Baker, and the two women had made the house into a sort of refuge for intellectually minded women.

"Is anyone else here?" Jane asked, glad of the change of subject.

"The twins and their Aunt, Miss Devoy and Olive -I mean her Grace - is in residence at Pemberton Hall."

"Olive is here?" Jane squeaked, near spitting out her tea in excitement at the news that her closest friend was nearby.

"Aye, his Grace attended one ball in London,then declared his season over," Polly said with a snort of laughter. "She said he prefers the company of the cattle in the fields to the cow-eyed cretins in Town."

Jane could well believe it. Although she, and many of his friends, knew that he had not murdered his previous wife, there were still many members of the ton who believed that the Duke had. Suspicious eyes followed him wherever he went, who could blame him for wanting to return home to the peace of Cornwall?

"She'll be here this evening," Polly continued, standing up to clear away the now empty cups. "Pop down after supper, everyone will be delighted to see you."

Polly began to bustle around the kitchen, clanging pots and pans, which Jane took as her cue to leave. With a heavy heart she set off up the road to Jarvis House, which lay just outside the village. The servants were thrown into a tizzy when they saw she had arrived.

"Oh, Miss Jane," the housekeeper wailed, "You should have sent word. The house in a state - we're not fit to receive a future Duchess."

"I'm no longer going to be a Duchess Mrs Lacey," Jane said with a sigh, "So, please don't fret. Can you have one of the girls set a fire in my room and draw me a bath. I'm bone tired after my journey."

Ignoring the woman's open-mouthed shock at the news that she would no longer be marrying Lord Payne, Jane made her way up to her bedchamber. She removed her dress unaided, before flinging her weary body onto the soft feather mattress.

I'm not going to be a Duchess, she thought, Nor shall I marry Alastair. I'll be a spinster for life. And worse, she realised with a gulp, she would be a homeless spinster once Julian uncovered her duplicity.

"Oh, look it's Jane!"

Poppy, or Alexandra Jane wasn't quite sure which, leapt up with excitement as she let herself into the drawing room later that evening. Every head turned to face her and Jane found herself looking at the warm, welcoming faces of some of her closest friends.

"I thought you'd have abandoned us, now you're to be a Duchess," Mrs Actrol, the grey-haired authoress, called with a cackle of laughter.

"Yes, we thought you'd be far too busy hob-nobbing with the upper crusts, to bother with us," Petronella Devoy added, with a wink. As the daughter of a Viscount, Petronella was as part of the aristocracy as Jane was.

"If an actual Duchess has deigned to spend the evening with us," Polly sniffed in a faux haughty manner, "Then a Duchess in waiting should consider herself honoured to be invited to this prestigious event."

The room fell into gales of laughter and even Jane, morose though she was, felt the corner of her lips tug upward. The boarding house was such a mixture of characters, both titled and not, and yet the atmosphere was one of warmth and welcome. If only she had stuck with Payne's initial plan, she might be here telling her friends that she had saved the house from being sold.

"The only problem is," Jane said delicately, once the laughter had died down, "Is that I am no longer going to be a Duchess. I shall remain plain Jane Deveraux, I'm afraid ladies."

Olive met her eyes with a worried glance, while the rest of the women rallied around her, uttering words of comfort.

"You are many things Jane, but plain has never been one of them," Mrs Actrol boomed loudly from her seat.

"Thank you," Jane smiled, then catching Olive's eye, she added, "Why don't you allow a Duchess and a nearly Duchess fetch you ladies some tea. Then when I get back, I want to hear all about what has been happening in my absence and Mrs Actrol's newest work."

Jane hurried out of the room, with Olive hot on her heels.

"What happened?" her flame haired friend asked, once they were alone in the kitchen, away from prying ears. "I thought that you were to keep the pretence up for the whole of the season? It's barely been a fortnight."

As she filled the kettle with water and placed it on the hob to boil, Jane told Olive, in a calm measure voice, exactly what had happened.

"So, you were right," she finished, her voice quaking slightly, "Alastair was nothing but a slimy slug."

"Oh, dear," Olive reached out and placed a comforting hand on Jane's arm. "I wish I hadn't been right about him. Still - it's best you know now what an odious creature he is. Rather than in two years time when he had disappeared with your dowry."

"Yes, everything has worked out perfectly," Jane chirped a little manically, "Except I'm right back at where I started. Single, dependant on my brother and without a penny to my name. Do you know has Mr Sneak taken up the living yet? He might be my last hope for a roof over my head."

"Now, stop that," Olive said sternly, "You will always have a home with me, and Julian will not turn you out on the street. Besides, a woman of your learning could find employment as a governess - or even a companion if needs be. You are not destitute Jane, far from it."

Olive's words, delivered in her usual assured manner, were deeply comforting, apart from one thing:

"Oh, no. Belinda!"

At the mention of companions, the blonde haired woman had popped into Jane's head. She had fled Hawkfield Manor without telling her companion she was leaving. Lord knows where the young woman had ended up.

"I'm sure she'll be fine, Jane, don't fret," Olive said, taking the whistling kettle off the stove and pouring the boiling water into the waiting tea pot. "What I'm most concerned about is poor Lord Payne."

Jane felt a stab of guilt at the mention of his name and remained silent.

"You fled his house and he has no idea where you are," Olive continued, fetching several cups and a tray. "He probably thinks that Mr Jackson has kidnapped you. I hope he doesn't call him out."

"He wouldn't," fear wracked Jane at the thought of James facing down a pistol for her. How would she live with herself if he died -and all over a stupid misunderstanding.

"He might, you know how impetuous he can be," Olive said with a sigh. She turned to look at Jane, her green eyes knowing. "And if he did? What would you do?"

"Why," Jane stuttered, "I'd throw myself bodily in front of him and beg him not to put his life at risk. I couldn't bear the thought of a life without James."

"Is that so?" the Duchess gave a smirk and deftly lifted the heavy tray, "Then perhaps you are more fond of Payne than you realise. Do you know Jane, for such a clever woman, you can sometimes be very silly."

That was the second time in one day that someone had pointed that out, and Jane was starting to think they were right.

16 CHAPTER SIXTEEN

"Are you quite certain that Jane would have come to Cornwall?" James asked Miss Bowstock, for what was probably the millionth time on the journey.

"Quite certain," she replied tetchily, her gaze returning to outside the carriage window. The journey to Cornwall had been long and arduous for the four occupants of the carriage. Upon finding Jane gone, James had wanted to head straight for London, where he was sure that he would find Jane held captive by the odious Mr Jackson. It had only been Belinda's intervention, and her insistence that Jane had fled to St Jarvis, that had stopped him.

"What makes you so sure?" he had asked, all those days ago.

"Well, she was a trifle upset about that incident in the library. The one where you punched Mr Jackson in the face," Belinda had whispered. "And she said that more than anything she longed to be back in St Jarvis. So I can only assume that was where she went. Besides, my Lord, if she was being kidnapped she would not have had time to pack."

And so James, Belinda, Caroline -who had insisted that she chaperon Belinda, and the Marquess of Falconbridge had set off at once. The Viscount and Viscountess Jarvis had opted to travel separately, owing to Emily's delicate condition, which suited James just fine, as Julian was acting like a boar with a tummy ache of late.

Three days later they were nearing St Jarvis and nerves were frayed, to say the least. James had no idea what had transpired between Miss Bowstock and the Marquess of Falconbridge, but the girl did nothing but avoid his eye, while he did everything to try and catch hers. It was exhausting watching the pair of them.

"We're nearly here," James said with relief, as the carriage turned onto a familiar coastal road. Despite his anxiety, he took a moment to appreciate the beauty of the view. The Cornish sky was blue and cloudless, whilst the sea glittered and winked beneath it. The countryside was in full bloom, daises and cowslips peered out of the hedgerows and even the grass seemed greener here.

"It's beautiful," Miss Bowstock breathed, her eyes lighting up as she absorbed the splendour of the view. "I have never been to the seaside. My father always promised he would take me, but he never got a chance before he—"
She stopped speaking abruptly, her face slightly paler than before.

"I did not know your father had died, Miss Bowstock," the Marquess said gently, his first words in nearly a day. "My condolences for your loss."

"Thank you, my Lord," she responded, bestowing upon him a swift, cursory glance. James watched the exchange subtly, certain that something had transpired between the pair. Oh, well, if it had, he was sure it would all come to light in due course.

"Tell me we have nearly arrived," Caroline said with a yawn, the conversation having woken her from her slumber.

"Nearly," James answered curtly, they were about an hour's drive from St Jarvis by his estimates.

"And what is the plan once we get there?" his sister questioned, her eyes now awake and curious.

"Ah…"

Therein lay the issue with their current adventure. What James really desired to do was to get to St Jarvis, sweep Jane into his arms and insist she marry him there and then. However, as he had pointed out to Caroline, he had wanted to win Jane's heart, her whole heart. He could not make her marry him, no matter how much he desired it. And he could not marry her, knowing that he was only second choice.

"I owe Jane a large sum of money for agreeing to pretend to be my betrothed," James said with a shrug, ignoring Falconbridge's raised eyebrows, which were in danger of disappearing through the roof of the carriage. "She wanted to buy the boarding house. If that is still what she wants, then that is what she shall have."

"You're setting her free," Miss Bowstock stated, her eyes wide as she marvelled at his words. "Oh, how romantic."

How consigning himself to a life of lonely misery could be considered romantic, was beyond James, though he had never claimed to understand the mysterious workings of the female mind. Even his sister, who could usually be counted upon to be cynical, looked slightly misty eyed.

"What utter tosh," Falconbridge put an end to the lady's romanticism. "If you love her, then you must fight for her Payne. Just a few days ago you were ready to put a bullet through Jackson for her hand."

"Jackson's not the obstacle any more, though," James shrugged, "It is Jane herself -and you can't suggest I put a bullet through her."

"No," Falconbridge retorted, "Though you can ruddy well tell her that you want her as your wife and that you won't take no for an answer."

Falconbridge finished this sentence with a pointed look to Miss Bowstock, who flushed and turned her head away quickly, once more affecting an interest in the passing countryside. The quartet spent the last hour in silence, each ruminating on their own predicaments, bar Caroline who fell back into a deep sleep.

"We're here," James leaned forward in his seat as the carriage turned into the driveway of Jarvis House. It had barely rolled to a halt before he opened the door and leapt out, taking the sweeping steps to the front door two at a time in his rush to get to Jane.

"Lord Payne," the butler gasped, as James came flying through the front door, "We were not expecting you."

"Where is Miss Deveraux?" James asked, too anxious for social niceties. "I must speak to her at once."

"She's not here," the butler replied, eyeing him nervously. James supposed he looked rather alarming, his clothes rumpled from travelling and his eyes wild with urgency. "She'll be down at the boarding house, if she's anywhere. Are you staying Lord Payne, if you are I'll have the rooms made up for you?"

"Yes, please," James called over his shoulder, for he was already half way out the door, running toward the boarding house and the woman who held his heart.

"You must be Lord Payne," a flaxen haired woman with a Northern accent opened the door of the boarding house, summoned by James' furious banging.

"Is Jane..?"

"She's in the parlour with the other ladies," the woman, who James presumed was the proprietress Polly Jenkins, said with a wide smile. "Come in, I'll show you the way. Though I warn you - anything you have to say will be said in front of an audience."

James did not care if he had to speak in front of a hundred people, he needed to see Jane and tell her how he felt. Though when he entered the drawing room and saw several pairs of feminine eyes watching him with undisguised glee, he nearly reconsidered.

"James," Jane stood up from her seat, her mouth open in shock, "I mean Lord Payne, we were not expecting you."

"I wanted to —I wanted to—" James stuttered, trying to frame what it was that he actually wanted to say, finally settling upon; "I wanted to tell you that I love you Jane."

A collective sigh went up around the room, as every lady's eyes swivelled from James to Jane, to gauge her reaction.

Jane stood stock still, her eyes blinking behind her spectacles. Dash it, James thought, I've frightened her.

"I know that initially our agreement was that you would end our engagement the owner of this fine establishment," he continued, "And if that is how you want this engagement to end, dear Jane, then that is how it shall. All I want is for you to be happy, even if it means that I shall be miserable."

"Oh, how darling," one lady from a pair of identical twins,

squeaked. James shot her an annoyed glance; there would be time enough to dissect his speech when he had left brokenhearted.

A silence filled the room, only broken by the arrival of Miss Bowstock, Caroline and the Marquess, as well as the Viscount and Viscountess Jarvis. They crowded into the already packed parlour, peering nervously between Jane and James.

"What did we miss?" his sister asked in a loud, stage whisper. James cringed —trust Caroline to be so direct.

"Lord Payne has told Jane that he loves her and wants her as his bride," Polly deadpanned, "Though he is willing to let her go, if that is what will make her happy."

"No. No. No."

James jumped, as Julian gave a growl of annoyance.

"You shall accept Payne's proposal Jane, or find yourself without a home," the Viscount threatened, "I shall not have a spinster sister foisted upon me for the rest of my days."

"Yes you shall," a small voice called, interrupting the Viscount mid-speech. To James' surprise it was Emily who had spoken, her face flushed with annoyance. "Jane is my sister too Julian and she will always have a home with us. Though why she'd want to stay with a bad tempered mule like you is beyond me."

James raised his eyebrows; it was nice to see Julian finally being brought to task.

"So, there you are Jane," he said, breaking the silence that had again fallen, "Every option is open to you. You can choose any path you like."

It felt as though the whole room was collectively holding their breath, waiting for Jane to speak.

"I..," she began, and James felt as though his heart would stop beating completely as he waited for her answer.

17 CHAPTER SEVENTEEN

"I.." Jane felt her voice trail off and she struggled to quell her nerves. She had spoken in front of an audience before, though only on academic subjects and this was anything but.

"I," she continued, avoiding the eyes of her audience and focusing only on James. He was heartbreakingly handsome, despite his dishevelled appearance. "I have been told many times over the past few days, my Lord, that for a clever woman I have been acting very stupidly, when it comes to you."

He said nothing in reply, merely remained where he stood, his tawny eyes filled with hope.

"And they are right," Jane continued, holding his gaze with her own, "I have been completely an utterly stupid and blind James. It has always been you. You have always been my protector and my saviour —and when I try to imagine a life without you…It's impossible."

"So you?"

"I will marry you. I will love you for the rest of our days and I will be proud to stand at you side, as your Duchess."

For one unbearable moment, nobody spoke, and Jane feared that James would respond by telling her to go stuff a chicken, she had missed out on her chance. Instead, a wide smile broke across his face and he crossed the room in two long stride, before taking her into his arms and kissing her soundly on the lips. It was much tamer than their previous encounters, but it still left Jane feeling rather breathless.

"Behold my fiance," James called happily to the room, ignoring his sister's sarcastic call of; "Don't you mean behold her again?"

The ladies of the room stood up and rushed to Jane, surrounding her and bestowing hugs, kisses and good wishes.

"It's so romantic," Alexandra whispered, clutching her hands to her chest.

"Congratulations Jane," a soft voice said. Jane turned and found Emily standing beside her, a shy smile upon her face.

"Thank you, for what you said," Jane whispered, engulfing

her sister-in-law in a warm embrace.

"No, thank you for being so kind to me, even when I was perfectly horrid," Emily replied, "We shall be fast friends from now on, won't we Jane?"

"We shall be more than that," Jane declared, "We shall be sisters."

The room was in an uproar, as every guest of the boarding house began chatting animatedly. Polly declared she would make tea and left the room, bustling Belinda, who had been hiding in the doorway, out of her way as she left.

"Is that you Hestia?" Mrs Actrol boomed, from her seat by the fireplace, squinting across the room at Belinda, who turned white as a sheet.

Hestia? Who on earth was that? Jane thought that maybe Mrs Actrol needed to buy some new spectacles and swept over to her companion who was still trying to look unobtrusive, with her back pressed against the wall.

"Belinda, I'm so sorry for leaving without you," she whispered, feeling truly contrite.

"That's alright, I probably would have done the same myself," the usually cheerful Belinda whispered back, her face ashen. "Though I did have to spend three days cooped up in a carriage with the odious Marquess."

Odious was not a word that was usually used to describe the dashing Marquess of Falconbridge, though when Jane glanced over at him, she saw that he was watching Belinda with a dark scowl upon his face. Goodness —what was it that had happened between the pair of them?

She never had a chance to ask the question, for a hand slipped through hers; James. He gave her a subtle wink and gently tugged her through the doorway, out into the quiet hallway.

"Alone at last," her betrothed whispered, his eyes soft as he gazed down at her.

"And properly engaged this time," Jane whispered, feeling suddenly shy in his presence.

"We won't be for long," James declared firmly. "Next Sunday the banns will be read for the final time, then the following Monday I shall make you my wife."

"And I shall be Lady Jane Payne," Jane realised with a snort of amusement.

"Until you become Jane, Duchess of Hawkfield," James reassured her, "Though I might warn you, my mother is will probably live forever."

"Oh, no," Jane groaned, "Your mother. Was she terribly annoyed that I had left?"

"Gosh, no," James said with a laugh, "She was more annoyed with me. She told me not to return unless I was bringing back a wife and grandchildren."

"I suppose one of the two will have to do," Jane laughed.

"And once we are wed we can get to work straight away on the second," James whispered, his head lowering to hers. He caught her lips in a searing kiss, gently pushing her backward against the wall of the hallway. His kiss was full of tenderness and promises, and Jane felt tears on her cheeks.

"Goodness, are you crying?" James asked, his face a picture of shock as he pulled away from her.

"Yes," Jane smiled through her tears, "Though only because I am so happy. I love you James, I just wish I hadn't been so stupid for so long."

"It's quite alright," James gave her a cheeky smile, "It's nice to know that you're sometimes wrong —otherwise you would be perfect to the point of unbearable."

With a growl of laughter he leaned forward and kissed her again, and they would have stayed like that had Polly not interrupted them as she made her way to the parlour with a tray of tea.

"Enough of that," she called with a cackle, "I run a respectable establishment here. You two will have plenty of time for that sort of carry on after the wedding."

They would, Jane thought happily as a blush stained her cheeks, they would have the rest of their lives together.

ABOUT THE AUTHOR

Claudia Stone lives in Ireland with her husband and sons. She is originally from South Africa, but after three decades of rain, she has finally adjusted to the Irish climate and is happy to call Ireland home. Provided she gets at least two sun holidays a year, of course.

Printed in Great Britain
by Amazon

44520532R00085